The Amish Homestead

Stephanie Swift

Published by Trellis Publishing, 2021.

This is a work of fiction. Similarities to real people, places, or events are entirely coincidental.

THE AMISH HOMESTEAD

First edition. July 12, 2021.

Copyright © 2021 Stephanie Swift.

ISBN: 979-8224732494

Written by Stephanie Swift.

THE AMISH HOMESTEAD

STEPHANIE SWIFT

Rebecca Yoder stepped out of the taxi and looked reluctantly toward the old homestead that once belonged to her grandmother and where she'd spent her childhood. As the warm summer rain fell softly from the heavens, she lifted her eyes to the sky and let the droplets cascade over her face. After spending five hours on a crowded bus and then fifteen long minutes in a cab that reeked of cigarette smoke, the last thing she wanted was to go inside her grandmother's house and be flooded with old memories.

The cab driver wasted no time in leaving, and when a loud boom of thunder rolled in the distance, Rebecca finally moved from her stance in the front yard to the covered front porch. An eerie stillness surrounded her, making her shiver as she pulled a rusty key from her suitcase and held it firmly in her hand.

Her grandmother had passed away almost six months prior, and Rebecca had put off the inevitable for as long as she possibly could, but it was now or never. As she slid the key inside the front door lock, she reminded herself that the sooner she finished tending to her grandmother's estate, she could be on the next bus back to Ohio.

The door hinges creaked and groaned in protest when she unlocked the heavy oak door and pushed it open. Because of the rain, there was no sunlight shining through the windows to light her way, so she was forced to fumble around the house in semi-darkness for a lantern or candle. She found a lantern in the kitchen, along with a box of matches, and she lit the wick as quickly as possible to chase away the chill that had seeped into her bones.

Rebecca carried the lantern from room to room and found two more lanterns and three candles, which she lit and scattered throughout the house. Before long, the unsettling, stale atmosphere was replaced by a soothing glow that made the barren home seem a tad bit more cheerful and welcoming.

Her late grandmother had been a simple woman with simple tastes, and it showed in the lack of personal items in the house, except for the quilting and knitting supplies that were neatly stacked in a corner of her bedroom and the Bible on the dresser by her bed. She used only the bare necessities, from her handful of cooking pots and utensils to the lone sofa in her living room.

She smiled as she pictured her grandmother sitting on the sofa, knitting a new bonnet and humming her favorite hymn, Amazing Grace, while she sat at her feet and did her schoolwork. After being abandoned by her mother when she was an infant, Rebecca's grandmother was the only real mother she'd ever known, and she'd never met her father. She didn't even know his name. Actually, no one did – not even her grandmother. That was a secret privy only to her mother, and after leaving their little Amish community – and Rebecca – when she was nineteen years old, all of her secrets went with her.

Rebecca walked from room to room again, mentally assessing how many items would need to be boxed up and moved before she could try and sell the house and, thankfully, there wasn't much to be found. Most of her things could be shared amongst the women in town, like her quilting supplies, clothes, and the few items she had in her kitchen. The furniture would be sold with the house, and whatever remained would be donated to Goodwill.

The only thing Rebecca knew for certain that she wanted to take back to Ohio with her was her grandmother's Bible. She went to her room to retrieve it, and she yelped when her shoe caught on something and nearly hurled her to the floor. Rebecca knelt down and set her lantern beside her and started running her fingers over the wooden planks to try and see what had almost tripped her.

She noticed a nail sticking up about a quarter of an inch from one of the planks, and when she touched it she discovered it was very loose and could be wiggled free. The nail at the opposite end of the board was also loose, and when she pulled it out and lifted the plank, her gaze widened in surprise when she saw several notebooks hidden in a small space beneath the floor.

Rebecca took them out one by one and set them beside her. There was a total of nine books, and the first one she picked up was filled from cover to cover with her grandmother's handwriting. From what she could tell, it was some type of journal, and her heart raced as she read the first entry, which was dated January 29th, 1998, the year before Rebecca was born.

The days seem so long now that Levi is gone. Anna is being rebellious again, and it's so hard with no one here to help me with her. Bishop Thomas believes I should just give her time to adjust to her father's death, but sometimes I feel it will only get worse before it gets better.

A tear escaped and slid down Rebecca's cheek as she reread the passage again and again. Her grandmother very seldom talked about her grandfather's death, and most days she had to plead to find out more about Anna, her mother. Perhaps now, with these journals, she would finally be able to put the pieces of her life together.

A knock on the front door startled Rebecca, and as she jumped up and walked quickly to the living room, she looked around for something she could use to protect herself, in case it was someone she didn't know. She picked up an iron poker beside the fireplace and held it close to her side as she unlocked the front door and slowly eased it open.

* * *

"You're not planning on using that on me, are you?" Joseph asked with a smile.

Rebecca blushed as she leaned the fire poker against the wall beside the door and ushered him inside the house before giving him a big hug. It seemed like an eternity had passed since he'd seen her, and she still looked just as beautiful as ever.

"I'm sorry," she replied. "I guess I'm a little jittery. How are you?"

Joseph took off his hat and wiped the raindrops from the brim before hanging it on a wooden peg beside the door.

"I'm doing okay. I was working in my barn when I saw the taxi pull into your driveway, and I just wanted to stop by and say hello."

That wasn't actually the truth, but he didn't want to just blurt out that he'd heard through the grapevine she was coming home or how he'd waited and watched from his living room window for her arrival all day long.

"I'm glad you did. Come on! I've got to show you something!"

When she suddenly grabbed his hand and pulled him toward the hallway, his heart flip-flopped inside his chest, and he was instantly transported back in time to their days in school, when they were eight years old and walked home every day hand-in-hand. Her skin was still just as soft and warm as he remembered, and he wished he could hold on to her forever, the way he should have the first time she announced she was moving to Ohio.

"You won't believe what I found," she continued. "I was in my grandmother's bedroom earlier, and I found a stash of diaries hidden beneath one of her floorboards."

He had to admit he was intrigued, and when they walked inside the bedroom, and he saw the numerous notebooks stacked on the floor, he went right to them. They both sat down, but Joseph couldn't bring himself to pick one up.

"Maybe I should just sit here and keep you company while you look through them," he said.

Rebecca gave him a curious look. "Why?"

He shrugged as he gestured to the notebooks. "I don't know. I just feel like I'd be betraying her trust if I read them. They're probably full of girly stuff anyway. She might not want a man anywhere near them."

She laughed softly. "I suppose you're right."

The sound of her laughter was music to his ears, and as he watched her by the dim glow of the lantern, he felt the irresistible urge to kiss her, something else he wished he'd been brave enough to do when they were younger.

"Do you think she wrote about your father in one of these?" he asked.

He noticed her demeanor change instantly, and he felt like kicking himself for even mentioning it, especially knowing how sensitive she was over her parents. She ran her fingertips over the cover of the notebook in her hands before giving him a half-hearted smile.

"That's what I'm hoping. I'm also hoping she wrote down her biscuit recipe in one of these. I still can't make them as good as she used to, and I couldn't pry that recipe out of her to save my life."

Joseph chuckled. "So, how long will you be in town?"

She glanced around the room and sighed heavily. "I'm not sure. Probably just long enough to empty the house and get it ready to sell."

He stretched his long legs out in front of him and crossed his ankles. There were a few things he'd recited in his head all day that he wanted to say to her, but he knew he needed to tread carefully.

"Have you thought about moving back home?" he asked.

Rebecca put down the notebook and turned to face him. She didn't say anything right away, and each second that passed made him more and more anxious.

"I don't know what I'd do here, Joseph. Since I moved to Ohio with my aunt Hope and uncle Elijah, I've been working with them in their farmers market, and I really enjoy it. I'm not sure how I'd earn a living here. I tried to find a job after my grandmother died, but no one would hire me. That's why I had to move in the first place."

He remembered all too well, and he still hated himself for not proposing to her all those months ago. He considered throwing caution to the wind and proposing to her right then and there, in that very moment, but he knew that would probably send her running back to Ohio, so he kept his mouth closed – for the time being.

"Anyway, let's talk about something else," she suggested. "How have you been? How is your family doing?"

He frowned a bit, not wanting to change the subject, but also not wanting to force her to talk about something she wasn't comfortable with. He leaned back on his hands and watched as she reciprocated between looking at him and thumbing through the notebooks.

"I've been staying busy between father's construction business and getting ready for harvest season. The family is fine. I'm sure they'd love to see you before you leave. Emily asks about you all the time."

She smiled when he mentioned his little sister, and the dimples in her cheeks made his heart race. She was such a stunning woman, but she had no idea just how beautiful she was, which was an endearing quality.

"I'll do my best to stop by and see them soon. Tell your mother I'll bring her my grandmother's quilting and knitting supplies. I remember how much they used to love making things together."

It made his heart swell listening to her reminisce, and he hoped she hadn't forgotten how close the two of them were once upon a time too. Then again, perhaps friendship was the only connection she had with him, since he'd never actually professed his love for her during the many years they'd known each other. For all he knew, she probably had a boyfriend back in Ohio.

Joseph shook his head and forced the troubling thoughts from his mind. For as long as he was able to, he would hold on to the hope that the two of them would someday be together.

* * *

Rebecca was having a hard time keeping her eyelids from closing. She'd spent the past three hours reading her grandmother's journals, and so far, she hadn't found out anything about her mother, other than the fact that she treated her grandmother terribly while she was a teenager, which made her both angry and sad.

She leaned back against the headboard on her bed and looked up at the ceiling. The rain had finally stopped and now that the incessant tapping on the tin roof was gone, the house was eerily quiet. She thought back to Joseph's visit and smiled. She'd missed him more than she realized, and it was so good seeing a familiar, friendly face. She should've been honest with him and confessed how much she detested living in Ohio, but she knew it would only make him worry.

She would gladly move back home if there was any way she could support herself, but right now she couldn't risk it. If she had time, she might go to Lancaster and inquire if there were any jobs available, but she wasn't going to get her hopes up again. Most of her Amish neighbors worked on their farms and there were very few jobs available for them in the city limits. Her job at her aunt and uncle's market was just that – a job – and it wasn't one she particularly enjoyed either.

Rebecca glanced at the clock beside her bed and groaned when she saw it was almost four in the morning. The sun would be coming up soon, and there was so much that needed to be done. If she wanted to accomplish any of it, she knew she had to get some rest. As she went to close her grandmother's notebook, however, she discovered a new name she hadn't stumbled upon yet.

I overheard a couple of English women talking about Anna while I was in the Williams' hardware store this morning. I didn't know them, but when they mentioned the owner's son was seeing an Amish woman with dark, curly brown hair, I knew they were talking about my Anna. It also explained why she's been asking to run errands in the city by herself recently. If this young man is the reason she's been getting into so much trouble lately, I'll be forced to confront his father about the situation. I hope it doesn't come to that, but I'll know more when I talk to Anna this afternoon.

Rebecca's heart started pounding as she reread the entry. She knew of the Williams' store, but she'd never visited it because her grandmother did business with another hardware store owner in the city. She always wondered though why she chose it instead of the Williams' store, which was closer, but she never questioned it. Maybe this was the reason why.

The next journal entry was dated almost one month later, which was odd considering her grandmother rarely went two days without writing something.

So much has happened I don't know where to begin. Anna and I are barely speaking now since the breakup, but I know it's for the best, and I won't let her convince me otherwise. I so wish Levi was still here. He would know what to do and what to say to make things better. I never realized how hard it would be raising a child on my own, but I know Gott will get us through this. He always does.

Rebecca kept reading, devouring every word, hoping that her grandmother would verify that the Williams' boy was her father, but there was nothing. She wrote about discovering Anna's pregnancy and the criticism she received from the community over being an unwed mother, but there was never a word about her father.

It made her sad thinking about the hardship they faced while she was in her mother's womb, but when she came upon the entries written after she was born, there was no denying how happy her grandmother was. Her eyes filled with tears when she read the entries detailing her first words and her first steps, but her mother was rarely mentioned again until the day she left home and never returned, when Rebecca was almost one year old.

My worst nightmare has become a reality. She's gone. Anna packed her belongings and left during the night, and I fear she may never return. My heart is broken...

Rebecca's mind raced in a thousand different directions, as she jumped from her bed and started changing clothes. According to her clock, it was now almost six, and she knew Joseph would be awake and preparing for work. She hated asking him for help, but he was the only one she trusted to keep a secret. Plus, he was the only person she knew of who would loan her a horse and wagon without asking a ton of questions.

She slipped on her socks and shoes and hurriedly brushed her teeth and hair before grabbing the notebook with the information she needed and racing out the front door. Luckily, Joseph lived only a couple of houses down the road because the rain had turned the main road into one big soggy mess. She nearly lost her footing a couple of times before making it to Joseph's, and by the time she arrived her shoes were caked in mud.

Rebecca climbed his front porch steps and removed her shoes before knocking on his front door. She tried not to sound as desperate as she felt, but when he didn't answer on the first try, she knocked on the door a second time even harder and louder. When he finally opened the door, she could see the concern register on his face immediately.

"Rebecca? Are you alright?"

She didn't know whether to smile or cry when she grabbed his arm and shook her head.

"I believe I know who my father is!"

* * *

Joseph thought he was still dreaming when Rebecca rushed inside his house and started talking about her grandmother's diaries, her mother, and something about a store in Lancaster. He'd barely had time to open his eyes when he heard the knock on his door and now she was pacing back and forth in his living room.

"Whoa, whoa, whoa," he said. "Okay, start over, but sit down first because you're making me dizzy."

She sat on the sofa, and as she flipped through the pages in her grandmother's notebook, he sat on the wooden coffee table in front of her and tried to focus on what she was saying.

"I found this entry about my grandmother overhearing a couple of English women in Lancaster talking about my mother seeing the

Williams' hardware store owner's son, but she never mentioned his name. Then she started talking about my mother's pregnancy, so I have a feeling this is him. This is my father."

She was so excited he hated to say anything that would ruin it, but he did worry she may be getting her hopes up over nothing. He vaguely knew the Williams family, but he couldn't recall anything about a son.

"Joseph, I really hate to ask this, but will you please let me borrow one of your horses and wagons so I can go to Lancaster and try to find this man? I would call for a taxi, but I only have enough money left to get me back to Ohio."

He couldn't find it in his heart to say "no", no matter how much he worried she may get her hopes crushed. Her beautiful green eyes were wide and expressive, and she looked as if she could literally jump right out of her skin.

"I tell you what, why don't you let me take you instead? The road is probably slippery after all the rain we've had, so you don't need to go alone."

She furrowed a brow. "I don't want to keep you from your work, Joseph. I'll be fine on my own. Really."

He shook his head as he stood and started tucking his shirt inside his pants. "*Neh*, the only way I'll agree is if you let me come with you. The wet roads are too dangerous, and you don't need to do something like this by yourself. I want to be there for you. I can catch up on my work when we get back."

She glowered at him and thrust out her chin, but he wouldn't be swayed, so she ultimately consented. Joseph finished dressing, and when they walked outside to his barn to fetch the horse and wagon, she got over her resentment quickly and started talking nonstop again. It was really quite adorable seeing her so happy and excited, and even though he was apprehensive about the whole situation, he did his best not to show it.

Perhaps this would end up being the most memorable day of her life and she would find the man she'd wondered about since she was a child. Then again, it could be a dead-end road, and she would end up hurt and disappointed and right back where she started. Either way, he would be there for her no matter what.

Joseph helped her climb into the wagon before taking his place beside her and grabbing the reins. The main road was just as hazardous as he feared it would be, so he had to go slower than usual, and there were a couple of times he felt the back wheels slide to the right. When they rounded the last curve and Lancaster came into view, he breathed a sigh of relief.

"I'm thinking about looking for a job here before I leave," she remarked. "It would ease the burden of trying to sell the house, and if this does turn out the way I hope it will, I'll definitely want to stay in the area."

He was elated to hear her talk about staying, but he did feel a bit disappointed that her reasoning had nothing to do with him. Still, if she moved back home that would be a dream come true.

"I think that sounds like a great idea. If you need some help, just let me know. I'll ask my parents if they know of anyone hiring."

His heart thumped erratically when he thought about having her within walking distance again and the possibility of starting up where they left off, but there was still one thing he wasn't certain about.

"Are you sure you want to leave Ohio? Is there a special someone you'd be leaving behind?" he asked.

Joseph kept his eyes focused on the road so she wouldn't detect anything in his gaze, but he heard her laugh softly beside him.

"*Neh*, there's no one special waiting for me, unless you count the tomcat that roams the alley behind my uncle's market who I informally adopted and named Sam."

Joseph threw his head back and laughed. "Well, if you get to move back home, maybe you can bring Sam with you."

She smiled at his comment before she covered her mouth with her hand and stifled a yawn.

"I'm so sleepy," she said. "I stayed up all night reading those journals."

Joseph patted his right shoulder. "Rest your head for a minute and close your eyes. I'll let you know when we get there."

It didn't take much prompting, and when she scooted closer to him and rested her head on his shoulder, he felt a warm rush of heat course through his veins. He could very faintly detect the scent of lavender shampoo in her hair, and he pulled up on the reins and deliberately slowed their speed so he could enjoy the moment as long as possible.

* * *

The Williams' hardware store was crowded when they arrived a few minutes later, and Rebecca looked around tentatively before heading to one of the aisle's. Joseph was right behind her, and as they made their way to the front of the store, he stayed on her heels.

An elderly gentleman was running the cash register, but he was much too old to be her father. At least, she hoped that was the case. He talked and carried on with his customers, and Rebecca noticed he had a kind smile that made him seem very approachable.

"May I help you?"

Startled, Rebecca jerked around when she heard the female voice and found a young woman who couldn't have been more than fifteen years old standing behind them. She was wearing an orange apron with a name tag clipped to it that read 'Williams Hardware' and 'Kimberly'.

"No thank you. We're just looking," she replied. "Could you please tell us where we can find the manager?"

Kimberly pointed to the man at the register. "That's him. Mr. Harvey Williams. He's the store owner and manager."

Rebecca thanked her as she walked away to tend to some other customers, and when she looked at Mr. Williams again, she was so nervous her hands started shaking.

"It's going to be okay," Joseph said. "You can do this."

She took a couple of deep breaths and moved another aisle closer to the front. "I want to wait until he's alone and most of these people are gone. Pretend like you're shopping."

They picked up a few items from the shelves and read the labels, and Rebecca glanced occasionally toward the register to see if the crowd was thinning, which it wasn't. She used that time to rehearse in her mind what she would say to him, but nothing she came up with sounded good enough. How do you even go about describing to a perfect stranger that his son may be your father? It even sounded ludicrous inside her head.

She placed a hand against her stomach to try and quell the mad swarm of butterflies that were wreaking havoc on her nerves when Joseph came up behind her and put his hands on her shoulders.

"I think it's time."

Rebecca followed his gaze to the register and she felt physically ill when she noticed Mr. Williams was finally alone and that the store was now almost empty. She nodded and swallowed hard past the lump in her throat before edging her way closer to the register.

"Good morning," he said. "How can I help you?"

Rebecca held her grandmother's notebook tightly against her body as Joseph nudged her in the side to coax her to speak.

"I'm so sorry. I don't mean to bother you, but I was just wanting to ask about your son."

She really hoped she didn't have the wrong person, and when he nodded, she felt her rigid muscles start to relax. He leaned against the counter, and she noticed his smile had faded somewhat, which made the tiny hairs on the back of her neck stand up right away.

"You must have heard about my Nathaniel," he replied. "Are you doing a report of some kind about the veterans?"

She and Joseph both gave him a quizzical look. "Veterans?" she repeated.

He turned and pointed to the bulletin board on the wall behind him, which was covered in photographs. He took down a photo and slid it across the counter to her.

"I apologize. I thought you might be doing an assignment for a college class about our veterans from Lancaster. Nathaniel's name is on the war memorial in the town square near the courthouse. He was a Marine."

It felt as if the air had been thrust from her lungs as she glanced down at the photo of a young man dressed in a Marine uniform. He had dark brown hair and looking into his green eyes was like gazing at her reflection in a mirror. There was even a hint of dimples in his cheeks.

"Was?" she reiterated.

The man nodded solemnly and sighed. "He was killed in Afghanistan several years ago."

She felt Joseph slide an arm around her waist, but she couldn't bear to look at him because she knew she would just break down in tears, and she needed to hold herself together.

"I'm...I'm so sorry for your loss," she stammered. "Do you have any other children?"

He shook his head before picking up the photo and replacing it on the bulletin board. "I'm afraid not. He was our only child."

Rebecca didn't know how to respond. The excitement she'd felt since early that morning was suddenly gone and replaced with the emptiest feeling she'd experienced since her grandmother's death. Mr. Williams spoke to her again, but his voice seemed distant as she stared at the photo on the bulletin board and memorized every little detail.

"Miss?"

Joseph squeezed her hard and she shook her head to clear her thoughts and focus on the conversation at hand. A couple of customers walked up behind them, and she smiled at Mr. Williams before moving out of their way.

"I do have some questions for a report I'm working on, but I'll come back later when you have more time, if that's okay," she said.

He nodded enthusiastically. "Of course, that would be fine."

She didn't trust herself to say anything else without breaking down in tears so she simply waved at him before backing away from the counter.

"Rebecca, I'm so..."

She held up a hand to keep Joseph from expressing his sympathy, which would only make her feel worse, and walked quickly toward the exit.

* * *

Joseph had never felt more helpless in his life. After visiting Harvey Williams two days prior, Rebecca had walked around in a daze and barely spoken to him – or anyone else for that matter. She'd stayed busy packing the remainder of her grandmother's belongings that she planned to give to Goodwill and getting the house spic-and-span and ready to sell.

After their visit to the store, she didn't mention anything else about finding a job in Lancaster, and he knew in his heart she had given up and decided to go back to Ohio. He tried to explain to her there was a chance Nathaniel Williams wasn't her father, even though he knew with one look at his photograph there was a very good possibility he was because the resemblance between them was uncanny.

He tried to convince Rebecca to go back and find out more information, but she refused to. Perhaps one day she would get the courage to return and explain to Harvey Williams who she was, but that decision was up to her. It was her life and her choice.

Joseph glanced out his living room window and saw Rebecca walk out her front door and place another box on the porch. He thought back to the last time she moved and how he'd stood by and let the same thing happen without saying a word, and he felt a sudden rush of adrenaline. He couldn't let that happen again – not without telling her how he felt.

Joseph left his house and sprinted the few yards that separated them and bounded up her front porch steps two at a time. Before he could knock on the door, she opened it and nearly bumped into him with another box in her arms. He grabbed it to keep them both from stumbling, and she peeked over it and smiled at him.

"Hey you," she said. "I'm sorry I didn't see you standing there. Short people problems."

He laughed as he took the box from her and set it on the porch. "Can we talk a second?"

She backed up and held the door open for him. "Sure. Come on in. I was just packing the last of the boxes before someone from Goodwill stops by to pick them up."

He nervously rubbed his hands together as he walked to the center of the living room before turning to face her. "I don't want you to go."

Rebecca put her hands on her hips and appeared genuinely confused. "I don't understand. Why?"

He filled the small gap between them until they were standing just a few inches apart.

"Please hear me out, okay? I should've said these things months ago before you moved to Ohio, but I didn't have the courage, and I refuse to let that happen again."

She nodded, and as she looked at him intently and waited for him to explain, he wished he'd rehearsed what he was going to say before rushing to her house unprepared. Joseph inhaled deeply and hoped for the best.

"I love you, Rebecca. I've loved you since we were eight years old and you let me hold your hand for the first time. I don't want you to go back to Ohio. I want you to stay here with me."

Her jaw slacked but no words came out, and before he could talk himself out of it, Joseph cupped her head in his hands and kissed her gently on the lips. He was afraid she might push him away and was beyond relieved when she didn't. Joseph released her and took a step back, and he could tell by the look on her face that she was trying to process what had just happened.

"Rebecca, all I'm asking is for you to please give us a chance. I want to take care of you and be with you – always."

She still seemed reluctant and confused, which made his heart sink.

"Kiss me again," she said.

At first, he thought he was hearing things, but he quickly did as she asked before she changed her mind. This time he kissed her longer and more passionately, and when they parted, he noticed the dreamy look in her eyes, which filled him with hope again.

"I'll understand if you want to take things slow, but I would marry you right here, right now, if you'd have me. I'd somehow get us to Ohio today and pack everything you own and bring it straight back to my house. All you have to do is say the word."

Rebecca smiled, and it was the first genuine smile he'd seen in two days, which made his spirits soar. She wrapped her arms around his waist and rested her head against his chest and Joseph breathed in the wonderful lavender scent in her hair before kissing the top of her head.

"One thing at a time," she whispered. "You know, my grandmother used to always hint to me that she would love to see us together."

Joseph grinned. "You've never told me that before. Why didn't you listen to her?"

Rebecca shrugged. "I don't know. I guess I worried I would lose your friendship if we courted and it didn't work out."

Joseph shook his head. "That would never happen. It definitely would've worked out. I can't think of a better way to start a relationship than as best friends first."

Someone pulled into the driveway and honked their car horn, and they both groaned when their perfect moment was interrupted.

"That's probably the mover with Goodwill," Rebecca said. "I tell you what, if you help me get the rest of these boxes packed and loaded on to the truck, we'll spend the rest of the day talking about our future and start making some plans."

Joseph grinned from ear to ear before kissing her one more time on the lips. "Deal!"

There was a knock on the front door and while Rebecca answered it and greeted the driver from Goodwill, he grabbed one of the empty boxes and started wrapping and packing the few items that remained in the house. He'd never felt so excited and motivated, and he couldn't wait to have Rebecca to himself so they could start designing the blueprint of their lives.

FROM

AMISH ASHES

TERRI DOWNES

Yet another argument, they thought, as it began.

"The gate's still not mended, Aaron? Just waiting for it to fix itself, are you?"

"You don't have to act like I've been sitting on my hands all day, Hannah. Simon had to leave and he took his tools with him. We finished everything else, in case you were interested."

"Oh good, I'm sure we'll be very grateful for the new window frames when all the sheep have wandered out into the lane. Nice to see you're thinking ahead, as usual."

Or, perhaps, they did not need to think of it as *yet another argument,* for to do so would be to acknowledge it as something out of the ordinary. The fact was, Hannah and Aaron would not have been able to think of the last time they had spoken without arguing, if they had been asked.

Some times were worse than others. This one seemed somewhere in the middle. Hannah was busy with the children, and never liked to be quite as sarcastic when they were around. The older ones might pick it up, she thought.

On the other hand, her mother was visiting, which never boded well.

"You'd think a man who has run his own farm for years would be capable of fixing a gate by himself," she offered from the kitchen table, as Aaron stood in the doorway with his arms folded and Hannah stirred at a pot on the stove with unnecessary vigour.

"Aaron mended it the last time, *mamme,* which is why it's broken this time," she said.

"And you know that for a fact, do you?" snapped Aaron. "There's never anyone who knows quite so much as the ignorant."

"Then you should be a walking library of information."

Aaron fell silent, as he so often did. Not a calm silence of retreat, but a dark, hot, hurtful silence. He gave as good as he got when he could, but he knew that silence drove Hannah mad; she could never manage to remain silent herself.

Hannah knew this as well, and knew that Aaron would remain withdrawn, forcing her to jab at him for a response. Turning her into the nagging, impatient wife and himself into a martyr, though he certainly would break his silence if he could think of a suitable retort. Her mother was still watching them, making her daughter so painfully aware that this was not how it should be. This was not how it had started.

Yet another argument, like so many others. Heat and ice in equal measures, both ready to burn. Hannah and Aaron each secretly wondering when it had become like this, between them. Neither willing to ask the question aloud.

This argument, however, was the first ever to be stopped by an utterly deafening clap of thunder right above the house, drowning out the words that had been about to be hurled.

It was also the first argument to be completely forgotten amidst the sounds of yells from the frightened children upstairs, shouts of "lightning!" and "fire!", and the sudden and pervasive scent of smoke...

Now, Aaron stood on the blackened floorboards and surveyed the space around him.

Eighteen years. Eighteen years' worth of memories had been stored in this attic, some from even beyond that, from his childhood. He should have been allowed a moment to mourn. But he could not have even that.

"Why don't you want the children to stay with my mother?" said Hannah, her voice cutting through the air still thick with the smell of burning.

"Don't start twisting my words, that's not what I said."

"Why else would you ask 'if it was a good idea'? It was generous of her to take them in until everything is fixed, and you know your parents don't have the space – "

"That's *not what I said.*"

Hannah hesitated. She knew that there was no love lost between Aaron and her mother; perhaps she should leave it for now, though she would not let him get away with that comment. For now – well, Aaron was no doubt upset over the attic burning, the loss of the roof and the damage to the outside of the house.

"I suppose," she said after a pause, "we're fortunate it was only the attic."

"Oh, yes, very fortunate," said Aaron icily. Was she not aware of how much effort and expense the damage would take to fix?

Hannah glowered at him, then turned and started picking at shapes in the ash at her feet.

"What are you doing?"

"Some of it may be salvageable."

Aaron almost laughed. "What could possibly be salvageable?"

"What do you suggest, that we just leave it here? Or throw it all away without looking?"

Aaron stared at his wife. For a moment, just a moment, he imagined doing just that.

Walking away. From all of it.

The thought seemed foreign to his mind even as it occurred. It was unthinkable, of course, to leave. The *ordnung* forbade divorce.

But how could this life, it one could call it that, be any part of God's plan?

All of this that had burned – had it ever been worth keeping in the first place?

He kicked at a pile of ash by his foot, raising a cloud of gray dust, and turned over a piece of wood with a hinge attached. It has half burned away.

"What would you suggest we do with this?"

Hannah looked down at the thing. "What is that?"

"Part of a beehive, I think."

"Oh, yes." Hannah rolled her eyes. "I suppose half of this place was filled with projects you never finished."

Aaron scowled.

"Oh, what?" said Hannah. "Is the truth so very offensive? You know you never finish your projects."

"Well who would, with you offering your *support*?"

"What do you mean?" asked Hannah.

She did not expect Aaron to reply. He never did, to questions like that. She still asked them, however, because if she didn't then it would be her fault for not knowing something. If she asked and he did not answer, then it was his fault.

Aaron looked at the charred fragment. And perhaps it was because of the fire, or because even losing all of this had not brought Hannah and him any closer, or perhaps it was because it was the beehive, of all things – he did what he never did. He opened up.

It was the last project Aaron would ever attempt from scratch.

He had never been that good at making things, he knew that. He started well, but somewhere along the line he would realize that whatever he was making did not look the way it was supposed to, and he did not know what had gone wrong.

Hannah always knew. He hated that she knew, that she was always able to point out the fault after he had failed.

But she wanted a beehive. She had always dreamed of making her own honey, of having sweet little bees tumbling in and out of the flowers she tended to with such care in the garden.

She would like it, Aaron thought. She was busy with their youngest, just born a few months earlier, and this would be a nice gift. He asked a neighbor for plans on how to build one, and had set aside a corner of the barn for the project.

He had been halfway done when Hannah had come to fetch him in, and saw what he had been doing.

He was annoyed, because the surprise had been ruined, but also because he was having trouble with the frames and she would be able to see. She would tell him what was wrong with them, the way she always did with everything he tried, as though she was being helpful, and he couldn't take it, he just couldn't –

"Those corners don't look very stable."

He had slammed down his tools and left without another word.

That had been four years ago. Aaron had not tried to make a single thing since.

There was a small part of Aaron which noticed that his wife's face looked softer than it had in years as she gazed at him across the ruined attic, her expression caught in the pale sunlight which filtered down through the fire-eaten holes in the roof. She was still able to catch him off guard, sometimes. After so many years, she was still the most beautiful woman he knew.

If only that were enough.

Another part of Aaron felt a sickening pleasure in the fact that Hannah seemed to finally understand what she had done.

"I'm sorry," she said. The first time she had said those words in so very long.

And if only that were enough.

"I was only trying to help," she said.

Aaron looked up in frustration at the charred timber above. "I know," he said. "You always want to help, and to fix what I'm doing wrong. You never seem to notice that your help doesn't actually *help*. All your criticisms and I never got any better, I just stopped."

Hannah bit her lip. Aaron deliberately looked away.

"You... you could still learn," she said. "If you're still interested, I know you always liked the idea of carpentry."

Aaron snorted.

"No, you could," she insisted. "You could work on this, fixing the house, maybe, if you worked with the other men they could teach you – "

"*No*," Aaron growled. "You're still doing it."

"But – "

"Just stop trying to fix me, would you? Stop, Hannah. Leave it alone."

Hannah watched her husband walk away, the way he did after – or during – nearly every argument. But this time, instead of feeling the usual burning rush of anger and a compulsion to follow him, to force him to speak, she felt something else. Something heavy and low-down. Sorrow.

What have I done? she wondered.

It was the next day when they returned to the attic. Aaron had wordlessly fetched some sacks in from the barn, and Hannah had brought up her oldest broom. She did not mention that Aaron had obviously conceded her point, that they needed to sort through the wreckage to see if anything could be saved. She felt uneasy about pushing him, today.

Not to mention the fact he was clearly expecting her to bring it up, and she did not want to give him the satisfaction.

She wished that his finally opening up to her yesterday might have changed something. He so rarely expressed his real feelings unprompted. It was one of the reasons she poked and prodded at him so much. If only he would be more open all the time, she would not have to force him.

The two of the worked solidly for a hour. Some tin trays were discovered to be useable and were put aside, as were a set of canning jar lids. Most items were unrecognizable.

"What is the point of all of this?" asked Aaron eventually.

Hannah remained quiet for a moment, unable to ignore the undercurrent to his words. But when she turned, she saw that he was holding up a small wooden item, badly singed.

"We clearly haven't needed most of these things in years. Why keep them at all? What was this, anyway?"

Hannah stared at the item. As the shape suddenly seemed to shift into something familiar, she felt a flickering at the base of her chest. Not a destructive burning, but the slow, sweet warmth of nostalgia.

"My letter rack," she said.

"Oh." Aaron looked down on it.

He had forgotten that in the first years of their marriage, Hannah had received so many letters from the friends she had left in her community at Goldacres that her sister had gifted her with her own personal letter rack.

"When did you stop using this, then?" Aaron asked. "And why keep it if you didn't need the thing?"

"A reminder," said Hannah. "Of... pleasanter times."

She almost stopped herself from saying it. But it was the truth. Aaron could not pretend that their life as it was now was worth commemorating. Indeed, he did not look as though he disagreed with her at all, although he frowned.

They had been pleasant, those first few years. Hannah had never been able to watch her tongue, perhaps, but there had rarely been anything hurtful that she had wanted to say. Aaron was not very expressive, but he had let his wife draw him out when she needed to.

"But you didn't need it anymore," he pressed on. "So..."

Hannah paused. This was not something she had ever wanted to share. But why not, when Aaron had already shared with her? She regretted that he had never told her sooner, of how her criticisms had hurt him. Maybe he should have.

Besides, she could not help but think, he was not the only one with a right to pain. He had hurt her, too.

"Another letter?" Aaron would ask whenever he found his wife reading one of her friend's missives.

She would nod, and smile, and share the news from Goldacres with him. After a while, he reminded her that he did not really know anyone from Goldacres, so she stopped telling him about what was happening with her friends. When he asked why she needed to write to her old friends so often, she stopped telling him when she had received a letter at all.

It took her a while to understand that Aaron did not have close friends as she did. He was mostly happy with his own company, but she could tell that he wished he had companions who would seek him out, and old shared stories, and in-jokes. He had always been a little left out, growing up. He was the youngest of his brothers, and they had been forever making him feel inferior in one way or another. Aaron had never been able to connect with friends the ways others had.

Hannah was the only friend he had, and he placed all his hopes on her. She was all of his company, all of his conversation, the only one who would share his past and present.

He was envious of her popularity. He would not say it, but even unsaid the fact remained between them, growing up like a hedge.

Hannah stopped writing her friends every other day. It went down to a letter every few weeks, then every couple of months. Then a handful a year.

The only exception was her mother, who wrote once a week regardless of whether she received a reply. Hannah sometimes wished that she would fall away in the same manner as Hannah's friends had.

Hannah made new friends in the community, but she was always aware that any time she spent away from the home, Aaron would be waiting for her, alone. She never stayed away too long, even as the years passed by and she began to dread the homecomings.

Aaron needed a few moments before he could speak. Hannah had not been able to stop, once she had started to explain, her words and sentences running together until they brought tears to the surface. Her tears normally angered him, as they were themselves often the product of anger, but these simply made him sad.

"I would never – " he stopped, wishing he could offer her his handkerchief, but he had used it to mop his sweaty, sooty brow. "I would never have asked you to do that," he said.

"Not in so many words," Hannah said into her sleeve, drying her face. "But I could tell that you minded, that you were left out. Is it so strange that I would have wanted to prevent that?"

It would have been strange now, she admitted to herself, though the thought almost felt like a betrayal of her own side during battle.

She felt tired, and wished there was somewhere to sit in the attic, but there was nothing. Even the floor was out of the question, unless she wanted to coat her skirts with black marks. So she remained standing.

"I just..."

Aaron slipped his hands into his pockets in the fashion he had had for as long as Hannah had known him. It was as familiar to her as any expression he had ever worn, his strong shoulders shrugging high, his head dipping. She wanted to cry again.

"I just didn't realize you'd care so much about that," he finished.

Hannah's mouth dropped open, even as she saw Aaron close his eyes in regret.

"I didn't mean that you – " he began.

"You didn't think I'd care?" demanded Hannah. "What on earth do you take me for?"

"I don't – "

"Maybe you see me as some kind of unfeeling villain now, Aaron, although goodness knows you're just as much in any fight as I am, but if you can cast your memory back to the time when we could actually stand being close to one another, maybe you'll remember how much I've loved you – "

She stopped.

I've loved you. Not *I love you.* Past tense, not necessarily present. Hannah felt the words as they came out of her mouth. Aaron would have felt them too, she knew.

But he did not say anything.

He went back to his work as Hannah, thoughts scattered, went back to hers.

Is that true? Do I not love him any more? Or am I just too angry with him to say the words aloud?

The quiet continued as they worked, through dinner, and into the evening. It was strange, Aaron thought, as they went to sleep that night, as far to each side of the bed as they could get, to have such real quiet. Normally it was him holding the silence in place, knowing that Hannah would force her way through it eventually. But now, with her not speaking either and no children to interrupt them, it was almost eerie.

Their room smelled of smoke.

The next morning, Aaron was anticipating Hannah breaking the silence. It was the last day they would be working in the attic, he thought. They had other areas of the house to see to.

He almost wanted to stay here longer. It was odd; the space was charred and ruined, an empty shell of no value. But the two of them had shared more in here in the last couple of days than they had in years.

Hannah was not looking at him. He watched her for a moment, looking at the strong, sure movements of her arms as she swept, how straight she kept her back. Her neck in particular, still long and elegant as ever. It had been the first thing he had noticed about her – her neck and throat. He remembered seeing her in front of him at Singing, when he went to visit a cousin in Goldacres. She had been unconsciously poised, her neck arched, swanlike, utterly arresting.

For the first time he could remember, Aaron broke the silence.

"You're still angry."

Hannah looked away. She reached down and picked up a parcel. The wrapping crumbled as she lifted it, revealing a pair of gloves inside.

"These are only a little caught at the edges," she said, as though she had not heard Aaron speak. "You could still wear them for work in the winter."

"Hannah – "

"Though I don't think I've seen them before. Do they not fit? We could save them for one of the boys, Henry maybe – "

"*Hannah.*"

She looked up, finally, her eyes blazing.

"Oh, I'm angry, am I?" she spat. "Because you think I don't care about you? That I never did, even at the beginning? Why would that make me angry?"

Hannah did not want to be angry. She could feel something had been happening between them, that some kind of ground had been covered. Now, she felt herself sliding backward, but did not know how to stop.

"You know I didn't mean it like that, Hannah."

"Oh, I know that, do I?"

Maybe they should just go back to the way it was. The way it had become. Maybe that was all there was, now.

But Aaron did not retort. He sighed, and slumped, his shoulders folding inward on his sturdy frame.

"Is it any wonder I keep silent so often?" he said, tilting his head to the side. "When anything I say has such power to hurt you?"

Hannah laughed harshly. "That's not why you stay silent," she said. "You stay silent because speaking gives me the power to hurt *you*."

She caught Aaron's surprised expression and shook her head. "You know it," she said. "I know it. Let's not lie to each other any more."

Aaron remained still in his posture of defeat. "When did things get like this?" he asked. "When – "

He looked down, and spied something glinting. Picking it up, he recognized it, and almost laughed himself. Of all the things to see at this moment.

He held it out.

"When did things like this start happening?" he asked.

Hannah stared at the cracked jug in his hand.

It was the first time she hadn't defended him.

Hannah's mother had never liked Aaron, and had never made a secret of the fact. She was not openly hostile, not yet, but everything she said and did around him was unavoidably tinged with disdain. She considered him to be unworthy of her daughter, poor at farming and unintelligent.

It was a few years after they had started fighting regularly, but Hannah was still protective of Aaron. She would never let her mother go too far with her comments. She would often bring them back up in private, but would always help Aaron to save face in the moment.

The jug, however, had been a gift from her mother. A family heirloom, given as a wedding present. Aaron had reached across the table too quickly and knocked it over, chipping the top and cracking the handle.

Hannah's mother had been deeply, bitingly sarcastic, the way that Hannah would someday become herself. And Hannah, instead of pointing out that the jug was still useable or that it could have happened to anyone, had sat in silence. She had betrayed him.

"It was the first time I realized how stupid you must think me," said Aaron bitterly. "How you must have agreed with your mother."

"I – I didn't," said Hannah.

"Oh, really?"

"You don't understand."

"Then tell me, why don't you?"

Aaron was once more struck by how strange it was that he was taking Hannah's normal role. But something strange was going on here – Hannah was staring at the jug as though it were a memory of something more.

"*Tell me,* Hannah."

She told him.

She had always defended him. Always. Her mother had not wanted her to marry him, and had been furious with Hannah's father for giving his permission.

"You're too good for that fool, can't you see that – You'll end up like me, with your dolt of a father – The boy's not even from the same community as us – Why would you go so far away from me –"

Hannah had never seen her mother like this. She had never fought her mother over anything before.

And they had fought, fierce and long, day after day. Hannah had frightened herself, learning what she was capable of saying and doing in anger – and, when her mother had suddenly shut herself off, refusing to speak to her daughter altogether – learning that there was such a thing as conditional love.

Perhaps the most frightening thing of all was learning how unhappy her mother had been all these years; that it was possible to be so unhappy and hide it, and that the idea of her daughter ending up like her had been enough to bring it all out.

"The jug was a peace offering, after all that." she said. "She didn't speak to me at all leading up to the wedding – I had to organize everything with my sisters, make the dress myself, she didn't help at all. But the morning of the wedding, she gave me her grandmother's jug. And I knew she had forgiven me, at least for the time being."

"I... I never knew." Aaron stared at the remainder of the cracked porcelain in his hands.

That was why her mother had been so upset. That was why Hannah had been unable to speak. He had not known any of it.

"You could have. You should have said something."

Hannah blinked at him. "How could I tell you?" she asked. "I knew how hurt you would be."

It did hurt, Aaron thought. But it was worth it to finally understand.

Something was filling him. Cooling him. It might have been sorrow, or sympathy, or just softness. He let out a long breath.

"Has anyone ever told you," he said, "that you might be a little overprotective?"

Hannah laughed. A real laugh, one such as Aaron had not heard in a long time. The corners of his mouth tugged up at the sound.

He reached across the space between them and passed Hannah the remains of the jug. Their hands, for a moment, brushed together.

It was not as though they did not touch anymore. They slept in the same bed, and lived in the same space. Touch was inevitable, and not something either of them really noticed any more. But this was different. Hannah felt every particle of her skin against Aaron's, as though her fingertips had been rubbed raw and sensitive. Aaron felt as though his hands were suddenly more connected to the rest of him than normal. He could feel the touch in the depths of his chest.

"I'm sorry," he said.

The next day, a work party arrived to help Aaron fix the damage to the house. Aaron had thought, when he had arranged it, that he would stick to the heavy lifting, taking on as much as he could to let the more skilled men do their jobs. But when Hannah stopped by at mid-morning to provide drinks for them all, he caught her glancing at him.

She lifted her eyebrows, and smiled. Just a little. Then nodded toward Johan Lapp, the carpenter who was doing most of the planning.

Aaron nodded in response and, after Hannah had left, went over to Johan and quietly asked him whether he might be willing to give a little instruction in return for more direct assistance.

"I'll learn as we go."

"Of course – nothing like knowing you've done a job yourself," beamed Johan.

Hannah had paused on the stairs to listen, hoping.

It had worked. She had encouraged Aaron, quietly, and he had taken the hint and her advice from before.

She should have been filled with joy over this improvement. But the emotion flooding her instead was a dull, aching shame. It had been so easy.

Well. Not easy, but simple. Aaron had told her how he felt – perhaps something she should have realized anyway, but still – and she had amended her behavior. It had taken effort for both of them, and would take effort from here on out. But they could have reached this point so much sooner. What had they been doing, the last eighteen years?

She looked upward for a moment. Perhaps because she knew Aaron was in the attic, working. Perhaps because something was nagging at her, a suggestion that there was something heavenly at work amidst all the dust and ash.

Later that evening, she listened to Aaron telling her what he had done that day. He spoke quietly, matter-of-factly. Hannah could tell it was taking a lot for him to share, that he was risking her gloating over being right. It was taking just as much from her to stop herself from saying *I told you so.*

They managed it. Both of them.

Aaron worked the next day, and the next, on the house, with every moment he could spare from the farm. It seemed such a strange, small, even silly triumph, just trying a bit of carpentry, but it was a triumph. He knew that.

He and Hannah had remained quiet around one another, saying no more than they needed to catch each other up on their day. Almost too cautiously, maybe, as though they were strangers, but with a sense of gentleness and care. Neither acknowledged what they were trying to do, but it was obvious nevertheless. As Aaron rebuilt their home, they were rebuilding something else.

Or perhaps something entirely new.

And maybe it was because of this that the next time Hannah's mother came to visit, things changed even more.

Aaron heard her voice as he was about to enter the kitchen.

" – surprised he's trying this himself, you know what a mess he makes of things, and I'm surprised at you for letting him, Hannah. The longer this takes the longer I'm taking care of your children for you and though goodness knows I don't mind – "

And on, and on. Normally, Aaron would come up with a reason to head back to work for a while longer. Especially when he would inevitably Hannah joining in with the complaints. This time, however, he found himself hoping.

He stood still and waited. Praying. *Please, tell me I haven't been imagining this. Tell me things have really changed.*

"Don't talk about him like that, *mamme*, please."

Aaron's heart leaped.

"Why ever not? It's not as though you've been particularly precious about him."

Hannah cleared her throat. "No, I haven't. But I've been very wrong, *mamme,* in speaking about Aaron the way I have with you. He's my husband."

"I"m only too aware of the fact. You don't have to remind me – "

Hannah's mother fell silent when Aaron walked into the kitchen. Aaron did not look at her, but kept his eyes on Hannah.

Looking at her, really looking, he saw something he had not expected: relief. He found himself thinking of the story she had told, of how miserable her mother had made her before their wedding. Of the power she still held over her.

As happy as he had been to hear Hannah defending him as she used to, Aaron now felt angry at himself. He had been sitting back and waiting for his wife to protect him without considering that she might need protecting herself.

He turned to his mother in law.

"I would like you to leave," he said, before he could think better of it.

Hannah's mother gaped at him. "Excuse me, I –"

Aaron held up his hand in a halting motion. "You're upsetting Hannah."

"She's my daughter, and I don't think that after everything you suddenly have a right to – "

"She's my wife," said Aaron. "And we're trying to fix things between us. This isn't forever, really, but for now you're just going to make things more difficult. For now, you need to leave."

Hannah's cheeks were wet as her mother slammed the door on her way out.

"Aaron," she said. "She's not –"

"I know," he said, sliding onto the bench opposite her at the kitchen table. "She's not the villain."

She was just one more thing they had allowed to come between them. One more hurt person in the world.

"Maybe we can help her," he said. "But we have to help ourselves first."

He laid an arm over the table, reaching out.

Hannah took his hand. She was not sure if he realized, but Aaron had been the first to say out loud what they were trying to do.

The work party kept at it for another week.

Hannah cleaned and aired the rooms, ridding them of ash, washing and re-washing every sheet and shirt until they were free of the scent of smoke.

Every night, she and Aaron found something to talk about. As each night passed, they managed to talk for longer.

Aaron started to reach for Hannah's hand as they sat before the fire in the evenings, they way he used to. It felt familiar and foreign all at once, almost uncomfortable to start with. It grew more comfortable every day.

On the last day that the work party came to the house, one of the men brought a package that Aaron had asked him to pick up at the store. Aaron said nothing in response to Hannah's curious looks, waiting until everyone had left that afternoon before giving it to her.

She nearly cried when she opened it to find a set of writing paper and envelopes.

She sat in the front room that evening and wrote two letters, to friends she had not spoken to in years. Aaron could not hold her hand as she did so, but he sat angled toward her, and every time she looked up she caught him gazing at her.

"What is it?" she said eventually. "You're distracting me."

"You're distracting *me*," returned Aaron, and Hannah felt herself blush.

"Oh, please," she said dismissively.

"I'm serious," said Aaron.

Hannah rolled her eyes and Aaron fell silent. After she had finished her letter, however, he spoke again.

"You asked me about those gloves," he said. "The ones I never wore."

"Oh, yes." Hannah moved back to the seat next to his. "Why didn't you, you never said."

Aaron sighed. "I never wanted to. They were a joke."

His brothers had always laughed at him, growing up. Maybe he had been more sensitive than he needed to be, but it had been hard to tell when it was in good humor or when it was just cruel. They had joked that he had needed to go to another community to find a girl who would take him after he had announced his engagement to Hannah.

Seeing her for the first time had shut them up, however, and Aaron could still remember how pleased he was, how proud.

But then the teasing had started again. About how he would need to look sharp and make something of himself, or else people would think there was something wrong with Hannah for choosing him. They had bought him an expensive pair of gloves, and said maybe they would help him to appear successful. As though he would not be insulted at such a suggestion of worldliness.

He should have laughed it off. He should have reassured himself that Hannah knew her own heart. Instead, pride had hardened, pleasure had become something to defend, and he had become almost afraid over how badly he wanted Hannah, that this just gave him more to lose.

"And I realized," he said, "that somewhere along the way I stopped telling you how beautiful you are. As though admitting it might remind you how many people thought you were too good for me."

Hannah had been staring into the fire as he had spoken. He recognized her expression easily. She was angry, but not at him.

"It's so stupid," she said. "How could no-one see what you are? How much you're worth?"

Aaron shrugged, embarrassed. Hannah looked at his shoulders as they rolled. "Not that much, really."

"No, you don't understand what I – " Hannah stopped.

She took a moment. Her voice had been rising once more, she had been going backward, back to where they had been. She could not do that.

But she could not let everything go, not when it was important.

She closed her eyes for a moment. *Lord, help me. I have to be able to talk to him. We have to be able to help one another without hurting one another. Help me.*

"You need to value yourself more," she said. "I think you – you're maybe more defensive than you need to be because you don't. If you knew how much you were worth, you wouldn't have to worry about how others see you. How I see you."

Aaron was silent for a long moment. Hannah felt her breath catch in fear, wondering if she had undone everything they had rebuilt.

He looked at her. He was not smiling. Yet he did not seem to be angry. Hannah reached out, tentatively, and took his hand. He squeezed hers in return.

"Thank you," he said.

For a moment, Hannah thought he was talking to her. But no – this was better.

"Thank you, Father, for the work you have done here," he said. "Thank you for the fire that came and allowed us to heal, and for helping us to rebuild. Forgive us for our failures, and for when we'll fail again. We know that you will be there guiding our steps and showing us the way."

They sat a while longer, in prayer. Then in silence.

We've come so far, thought Hannah, as they rose from their chairs to turn in for the night. It was not quite as it had been, of course. But they were holding hands, praying together. Perhaps everything else would come later. They had already had so many small miracles; the items they had found, the hurts that had been revealed so that they could be tended to. She should not ask for too much.

But then Aaron paused in the doorway and turned back.

"Oh, I nearly forgot – " he pulled something from his pocket. "I found these as we were finishing up in the attic. I meant to ask you if they were from anything. I mean, they just look like stones, but why would they have been – "

Hannah started laughing.

"What is it?"

"You don't remember...?"

Hannah had been half-expecting Aaron to disappear as soon as the ceremony had been concluded. He had never liked crowds, and even though her mother had promised to be nice, Aaron was sensitive enough that he could tell when someone disliked him.

So when Hannah had noticed her new husband's absence after the meal had been served, she had not worried, but had gone to look for him. She had found him skipping stones on the pond at the end of her family's garden.

He had smiled at her approach, lighting up with recognition, with the feeling that comes from mutual belonging.

"You've hidden long enough," Hannah had reprimanded gently. "It's getting dark."

"Just another minute – I have a few left," he had said, showing her three stones in his hand.

"Oh, really?" she raised an eyebrow. " And what if I wanted them instead?"

Hannah stepped close as she spoke; closer than she normally stood to him. He looked down at her, realizing this at the same moment she did.

"Could I trade them for something?" he had asked, dropping the stones into her upturned palm.

His gaze had traveled to her lips. They had kissed, earlier, for the first time. But it had been in front of witnesses, and each had felt a little shy. It had been quick, almost chaste.

Hannah had smiled, then swallowed, perhaps still a little nervous.

"Oh, yes," said Aaron. "I remember. I can't believe you kept the stones."

"They're cracked from the heat; they must have been right at the very heart of it," said Hannah, examining them and sighing. "It seems nothing quite made it through the fire."

But Aaron was still smiling at her, and Hannah suddenly remembered what had happened next. Just as he had eighteen years ago, Aaron dipped his head and pressed his mouth against the side of Hannah's neck. His favorite spot.

Even the very first time he had done it, as she had thrilled at his touch, it had felt immediately familiar. As though that moment of connection had somehow supplanted all her ideas of home, and had shown her where she would belong from now on.

"I love you," Aaron murmured. "But you're wrong. We made it through."

end

CALIFORNIA DREAMING

MONICA MANN

44

"And where do you think you're going?" The voice was like whiplash and Marta froze in her tracks, heat warming her face at being, the guilt of being caught overwhelming her.

"I was just – "

"I know exactly what you 'were just' and the answer is absolutely not!" Marta turned slowly, thinking of what to say next. She averted her eyes from her mother's stern glare and hung her head.

"*Mammi*, he's my brother!" she pleaded. "I can't – "

"You can and you will! Do you realize how much he has disgraced this family with his choices? Of course, you do and yet you still insist on sneaking around to visit him. You're no better than he is! You know this behavior is forbidden, Marta."

"*Mammi* – "

"That is enough, Marta. You must stay home and work on supper for the youngest. Your father and I have...something to attend to this evening." Bridget Chandler seemed to mimic her daughter's ashamed expression as she, too, glanced nervously at the floor. Marta nodded slowly, recognizing this was not the time to defy her mother. Since Frederick's devastating decision to leave the community, the strain on her parents had been obvious. While Marlin and Bridget had always had somewhat of a difficult time seeing eye to eye, Frederick's choice had impacted them both greatly, bringing their infamous bickering to an entire new level. Marlin was one to preach forgiveness while Bridget was apt to alienation and rejection. It was not a secret in their close-knit area that her parents were seeking the guidance of the bishop for their martial issues. Marta had done her best to maintain contact with her brother but it had become increasingly difficult since one of their neighbors had seen her leaving Frederick's apartment the previous month. The neighbor had quickly reported the infraction to her parents who had since kept a very careful eye upon her.

"The children are hungry, Marta," Bridget told her, sensing her daughter's reluctance. "They need you more than your so-called brother. Focus on the ones who are here and worthy of your attention."

Marta gritted her teeth to keep from retorting and removed her coat while her mother proceeded to adorn her own.

"And don't think once I leave this house you are going either," Bridget continued as she opened the door. "I have the Millers watching out in case you get some ideas in your head."

"Mammi! I am twenty-one years old! I do not need the neighbors to mind me!"

"That is enough! Watch your tongue. I wouldn't have to resort to such measures if you would do as you're told! Your father and I have enough woe without worrying about what silliness you're getting into, Marta. You have responsibilities here. Your brothers and sisters need you. Think of them before you go galivanting around town. Or are you leaving too?"

"No!" Marta felt a hot blush color her face. "No of course not! My place is here with you!"

Bridget snorted contemptuously, giving Marta a scornful glance as if she spoke venomous lies.

"Your former brother used to claim the same," she retorted before walking outside. "Look where he is now!"

She did not bother to say good-bye as she hurried off down the street to meet with Marlin and the bishop of the district. Marta stood watching her mother disappear down the lonely road and a mixture of feelings overwhelmed her. The days of pitying her parents were becoming less frequent and an uncharacteristic anger seemed to wash over her often. Some days, she felt as though her parents were taking Frederick's departure much too harshly and needed to focus on the positive in their lives. They had a thriving farm, four doting children and perfect health. It was Frederick's choice to live among the English and they had always been reared to understand that God had given them free will for a reason. Perhaps, one day when Frederick was older, he would return and become baptized as her parents so desperately desired but if he did not, it was still his life to live and his decision to make. The oldest Chandlers seemed to relish fighting above all else and Marta, the oldest daughter, was then forced to hold the pieces of their disintegrating family together. *Maybe Frederick has the right idea,* Marta thought, not for the first time. *Sometimes this is too much to handle.* Immediately, ashamed, she once again shoved the thought from her head and closed the heavy wooden door in the wake of her mother's bitter exit.

"Marta? We're hungry!" Little Levi, generally the spokesperson for the youngest children stood with his hands on his hip, half annoyed, half imploring at his sister. Marta sighed inwardly before forcing a smile and peering down at her small brother. He was unusually tiny for his six years but his personality more than made up for his frailty.

"Well then, I suppose I should make you some supper," Marta told him with cheer she did not feel. His frame, prepared for battle, seemed to relax and he turned to his brother and sister who stood behind him, waiting with anticipation.

"I told you she wasn't going to leave us here!" Levi told Simon and Melinda. Aghast, Marta stopped in her tracks.

"Why in heaven's name would you think something like that?" she demanded. Levi shrugged nonchalantly.

"Frederick left us," he replied simply.

"I am not Frederick, Levi. And Frederick has not yet been baptized. Sometime our young people need to go see the outside world to understand it before realizing how good we have it here," Marta told him gently, taking him by the hand. "You may find when you're older that you want to see the world before coming home too. There is no shame in that."

Levi accepted the gesture and the other siblings followed them as they retreated to the warmth of the kitchen where Marta promptly began to ready their evening meal.

"What about Caleb?" Levi demanded, flopping unceremoniously onto the floor. Again, Marta paused what she was doing to stare at her little brother.

"What of Caleb?" she demanded in a much sharper tone than she had intended.

"Caleb is baptized," Levi answered.

"Yes, he is." Marta began to feel a slight sense of unease in her stomach.

"And he wants to leave the community and move to California."

"Who told you that?" Marta was shocked. *How could Levi possibly know such a thing?*

Again, Levi shrugged his shoulders.

"Everyone knows, right?" He glanced at his brother and sister, who were both older but acted as if they were his shadow. They silently bobbed their heads in agreement.

"Anyway, so what if he does? What does that have to do with Frederick?" Marta was becoming irritated that her little brother was not only so well educated but that he was speaking circles around her.

"It has nothing to do with Frederick," Levi replied. "It has everything to do with you."

"How so, Levi?"

"Well, you're marrying Caleb, aren't you?"

"Levi, I believe that you need to focus more on your school work and less on the comings and goings of your elders. I have not agreed to marry Caleb. Why would you even think that I am going to marry Caleb?" Marta sighed, irritated that she was explaining herself to a six-year-old.

Levi grinned wickedly, realizing that he had struck a nerve with Marta.

"What are you smirking at, Levi?"

"Well I guess that's good news for Noah then, isn't it?"

"What do you know of Noah?"

"I know that he wants to marry you," Levi answered matter-of-factly.

Marta dropped the knife she was using and stared at Levi in disbelief. Her schoolboy brother knew more about her romantic life than either of the men vying for her hand did!

Marta Chandler had always been somewhat of a rebel. Her teachers called her a daydreamer and her father constantly worried that she would not be easily married off. Her will was strong and she did not adhere to the rules of Amish culture the way her peers and friends did. It was not that Marta did not appreciate their way; quite the opposite was true. Marta was smitten with their hard-working attitudes, unity to God and to one another. She adored the fact that her aunts, uncles, cousins and grandparents were so close in proximity. She took care of her siblings and tended to the farm without complaint or displeasure. The problem was, Marta had a ridiculously keen sense of fair play and when she felt something was even slightly askew, she was apt to point it out. This may have been ignored or even praised but for the fact that Marta was not exceptionally attractive. She often came across as an embittered woman when the truth was, she simply could not stand injustice in any form. God forbid if anyone was being berated or abused in her presence. Marta would set the perpetrator straight in seconds with a diatribe sure to ring in their ears for all of eternity. She did not possess a hot temper or nasty demeanor but a sharp, intelligent tongue. Even so, by the time she was in her teens, most of the children in her district identified her as "Meanie Marta." Marlin Chandler had been beside himself when he realized what kind of reputation his oldest daughter had gained for herself.

"Marta, you must not be so bold! It is not always your place to speak your mind!" Marlin had told her one day after a particularly embarrassing event at worship. It had been so humiliating in fact, Marlin had ushered the Chandler family into their wagon, forgoing lunch altogether.

"Someone had to correct him, *Daed*! He was making broad statements about people he doesn't even know!"

"Marta, I don't care if he was bathing them in boiling oil! He is the bishop!" But Marta stood firm.

"And I don't care who he is! In fact, that is more the reason for him not to utter such nonsense! Our community accepts his word as truth. There are impressionable children at worship! He can't speak that way about the English when he does not spend any time in their midst! Not all the English are Godless evil doers and he should not paint them as such!"

"Your love for your brother has clouded your opinion," Marlin sighed, shaking his head. Unlike his wife, he was much more mild mannered and while he was disappointed in Marta's brazenness, he did not speak harshly to her. Bridget, on the other hand, was antsy for her turn to reprimand her daughter when her husband was finished.

"Love does not cloud, *Daed*. Love takes the clouds away."

"You should focus more upon finding some of that cloud removing love, then, Marta and less time arguing with the bishop."

Marta said nothing but inside she was grinning to herself. She, the plain, mousy Marta Chandler, had not one but two men interested in her hand in marriage. At first, Marta had felt strange about being courted by two men but soon she realized that they had been brought to her as God's test. While they were both from her district, they were very different men. Caleb had grown up down the road from Marta's family and had been a dear friend to Frederick. Both boys had experienced their rumspringa together and while Frederick had opted to live in town, a mere hour carriage ride from their community, Caleb had decided to return and be baptized. Caleb had deeply mourned the loss of his best friend and Marta had been a wonderful supportive shoulder to cry upon in his absence. Inevitably, they became inseparable and soon found themselves sneaking off to hold hands and snuggle out of the sight of prying eyes. No one suspected anything but a platonic relationship between Caleb and Marta, everyone assuming that Caleb was simply taking Frederick's place in Marta's life.

It was for this reason that Noah felt safe to approach Marta unexpectedly one day when he discovered her browsing through the shelves of a bookstore in town. Marta had just come from a covert visit with her brother in his miniscule apartment over a garage of a minister's house. The kindly pastor had taken pity upon the clueless boy and allowed him to live in the unfinished room for a nominal rent while Frederick took a job as a barista at a local coffee shop. Marta had begun smuggling goods from home to improve the comfort of her older brother's surroundings such as linens, plates and candles.

"I have electricity here, Marta," Frederick laughed when she opened her burlap sack and dumped the goods upon his thin cot. "I have no need for candles."

"Oh hush! Candles are for romance! What if you meet a lovely English girl and wish to cook her dinner? That's what the English do, yes? Have their men cook for them?"

"Oh Marta! You are such a dreamer."

"Anyway, Frederick, I must say, you look much better in candlelight," she told him light heartedly. Frederick roared with laughter. Impulsively, he leaned forward and hugged her.

"Thank you, Marta. You are the best sister a man could ever wish for. I would have died if you had turned your back on me too."

"It is not too late to come home," she pleaded. "We all miss you terribly!"

Frederick shook his head.

"No, dear sister. That life was not for me. *Mamm* and *Daed* fighting all the time – "

"It has gotten worse since you left," Marta confessed.

"You see? How do you bear it? I cannot live like that. Anyway, they don't miss me. They haven't come to see me once since I came here. I guess I understand but I thought at least *Daed* would have come." Frederick pretended to busy himself putting away the items which Marta had brought and Marta felt her heart crack slightly at his longing for their parents.

"But enough about that. Look at this place! Neat, right? If you ever need to get away from all the chaos, you always have a home with me."

"Caleb misses you too, Frederick," Marta told him, trying to make him smile. Frederick arched a dark eyebrow at his sister.

"Oh? Do you see a lot of Caleb?" he asked knowingly.

"Here and there," Marta replied defensively but Frederick clucked his tongue.

"Be careful, Marta. You may find yourself living out of the community without an opportunity to return if you hitch your star to his wagon."

"How do you mean?" Curiosity got the best of her and she leaned forward.

"Caleb has big dreams. California dreams." Marta sat back, blinking. *California? Are there Amish communities in California?* As if reading her thoughts Frederick smiled humorlessly.

"There are none of our people on the west coast. He wants to become a comedian."

"Really?" Marta was not sure if she was afraid or intrigued.

"Yes. And what's more is I may join him on the trip." Marta's blood ran cold at the thought. *No! Frederick can't go away! He needs to stay here where I can visit! He is going to come home one day.*

As Marta left Frederick, she decided to see if he was right and investigate Amish communities in California. It was there where Noah found her.

"Hello, Marta," Noah said simply, poking his head around the corner. Despite his unassuming approach, Marta found herself jumping guiltily at the sound of his voice.

"Noah! Hello!" Her own voice sounded too loud and a pitch higher than it should have been. He smiled gently at her and Marta willed her heart to slow.

"I did not know you enjoyed reading," he told her, glancing at the history books she was searching. She nodded quickly.

"I, uh, I am just looking for some information on our communities throughout the nation," she told him truthfully. Noah's hazel eyes lit up.

"How lovely! We have such a colorful history. I'm sure you recall the lessons from school but we have over three hundred years of proud culture. It is one of my favorite subjects to discuss. Perhaps one day you and I can speak more about it?"

Marta was taken aback by the offer and she almost looked over her shoulder to see if he was speaking to someone else. Noah was considered quite a catch. He possessed all the virtues any woman could desire. He was kind, strong and very handsome. She found herself nodding vigorously.

"Yes! I would like that very much! How about right now?" she heard herself saying. *And what of Caleb?* A haughty voice in her head demanded. Marta shoved the thoughts from her mind and followed Noah from the store, the books she was seeking all but forgotten. *Caleb wants to move to California.*

"Marta!" She jumped as Bridget approached, the anger in the older Chandler's voice unmistakable. Marta wracked her brain, trying to pre-emptively recall what her mother had discovered her hiding this time. She turned away from the basin where she was doing the last of the breakfast dishes and wiped her hands on her apron. She took a deep breath to prepare for the impending lecture.

"Yes, *Mamm*?" Bridget narrowed her steely blue eyes and placed her hands on her hips.

"Is there something you would like to tell me?" she demanded. Marta swallowed and shook her head.

"No, *Mammi*. Why?"

"Where are all the candles I had in the woodshed?"

Marta felt the color drain from her face and she dropped her head, her long braids tickling her arms.

"I'm not sure, *Mamm*," she said evasively. "Are you certain you didn't put them somewhere else? Did you check the -?"

"I am quite certain I know where I put the candles I spent many hours making, Marta. You have no idea what became of them?" Marta shook her head quickly but Bridget clearly saw through the lie. Her blue eyes narrowed suspiciously and her hands found their way onto her hips.

"Did you take them to your brother? Don't fib, Marta!"

"I..." Marta did not know what to say. She would be in trouble no matter what she said. She tried to formulate a story.

"Try speaking the truth for once, Marta! I did not raise a liar."

"Leave her be, Bridget," Marlin Chandler walked into the kitchen and placed a cup in the basin of soapy water.

"How can you say that, Marlin? She has been stealing from our family to give to her rogue brother who abandoned us!"

"That is enough, Bridget." Marlin stared at his wife meaningfully and a look of fury washed over her face.

"You encourage this kind of behavior? Stealing and lying to your parents?"

Typically unperturbed by his wife's quick temper, Marlin suddenly developed a look of anger upon his face.

"I encourage loyalty and family values, Bridget. Something that has been taught to us since the dawn of time. It would do you some good to reach into your heart and remember the same lessons."

"So you condone this then?" Bridget was incensed and she balled up her fists. Marlin stood his ground and suddenly Marta felt herself retreating into herself. Her parents were fighting because of something she had done and she needed to put an end to it at once. They had enough with which to concern themselves without her adding fuel to the fire.

"*Daed, Mamm* – "

"Silence, Marta!" they both yelled simultaneously without breaking their angry glares at one another.

"I condone my daughter being a decent, loving human being, yes," Marlin hissed back at his wife. "If it does not mesh well with your holier-than-thou attitude, I apologize but I will not give Marta trouble for caring about her siblings!"

Bridget threw up her hands in disgust and spun on her heel.

"Then perhaps you and Marta should go join her fallen brother out with the English. Because you certainly share all their traits, don't you? Lying, deceit, thievery!" Without waiting for a response, Bridget stormed out of the kitchen and through the front door, angrily slamming it behind her. Marta started after her mother but Marlin stopped her, gently putting his hand on her arm.

"Leave her be," he told her. "She needs to let off some steam. Losing a child is extremely difficult Marta."

"But Frederick isn't lost, *Daed*! You make it seem as if he is dead!" she objected. "He could come back!"

Marlin smiled at his daughter's hopeful optimism.

"That would be lovely, *liebchen*. I hope he does." Yet Marta could hear the doubt in his words. As she watched her father retreat up the back stairs to dress for the day, Marta suddenly found thoughts of California pop into her head.

"Marta! Look at these!"

Levi tripped out to the field where she was chopping wood. Her breath was coming out in quick, steamy puff as she wielded the axe. Despite the incredible amount of energy it required, Marta particularly enjoyed cutting wood. It allowed her time to think, or as her teachers would say, daydream, uninterrupted. Before her tiny brother had arrived, she had been thinking about Caleb and Noah. She wondered which man would make a better husband but in her heart, she knew it would be Noah. He was constant and sweet. He was strapping and he was to inherit the family farm directly as he was the only boy among his siblings. He was also incredibly attractive, so much so that Marta was constantly amazed he fancied her at all with her mousy hair and too-wide eyes. While Marta enjoyed the time she spent with Caleb, she also recognized a slight laziness and surliness about him which she never saw in Noah. He was the youngest in his family and Marta suspected his parents had spoiled him more than his other brothers. While Noah would often ask Marta about her hopes and dreams, Caleb would spend hours talking about his desire to become a comedian and spinning dreams of California like webs in her mind without once pausing for breath or to let Marta speak. Often, Marta found herself feeling exhausted spending time listening to his desire to become rich and famous.

"Why didn't you go before getting baptized?" Marta asked once when she could get a word in edgewise. Caleb had shrugged his slender shoulders and sighed.

"I saw how devastated your parents were when Frederick left. I didn't want to put my family through the same. But now I know I made a mistake. I wasn't meant to live in this place. I was meant to be a star!"

"But surely you know what a difficult road you have ahead of you, Caleb. There are thousands of people who want to be stars in California!"

He had grinned disarmingly at her, squeezing her hand affectionately as if she had made the silliest statement.

"With you at my side, how can I lose?" he asked and Marta had smiled weakly back, feeling unconfident in his sureness.

Marta watched Levi trip through the snow toward her, holding something almost as big as him.

"Levi! Where is your coat? You'll catch a cold again!" she chided, dropping the axe and rushing toward the poorly dressed boy. Meeting him at the halfway point, he thrust the bouquet of flowers into her arms.

"What are these?" she asked, taking the wildflowers in one arm and scooping him up in the other. She wrapped her cloak around him and hurried toward the house. Levi had a history of falling ill and Marta was constantly worried for him because of his slight build.

"They are for you. From your husband-to-be!" Levi cackled gleefully. She shook her head in exasperation.

"And who might that be?" she asked, knowing exactly who he was referencing.

"Noah."

As they made their way into the back door, she gently placed her shivering brother on the floor before the wood stove, wrapping her cloak around his shoulders and placed the flowers onto the kitchen table. A wave of affection overwhelmed her as she stared at the gift/ There was no doubt that Noah would make the better husband.

"I have decided to go to California with Caleb, Marta."

A glass fell from her hand and shattered on the floor at Frederick's sudden announcement.

"When is this to happen?" she demanded, almost oblivious to the broken cup.

"Next month."

Gathering herself, Marta began to pluck up the big shards, her mind racing.

"You can't be serious, Frederick! What on earth are you going to do in California?"

Marta located a broom and began to clean up the mess at her feet, waiting for her brother to respond.

"I don't have to live in Ohio to pour coffee, sister. I can do that anywhere."

"But Frederick, what about me? Aren't you going to miss me?"

Marta saw him smile out of the corner of her eye.

"I won't have to miss you if you marry Caleb and come with us," he answered simply.

Marta said nothing, her heart hammering in her chest.

"Marta? Aren't you going to say anything?"

She bent over, her long skirt grazing the shards of glass as she swept the pile into a dustpan. Could she marry Caleb? There were worse men in the world, men who did not have the opportunity to keep her near her beloved brother. But what about Noah? Noah who wanted to remain in the comfortable, safe life which she loved. Noah, who would enable her to be among little Levi, Simon and Melinda. Noah who would allow her to care for her parents when they grew old. When she rose to her feet, Marta had decided.

"I suppose we are going to California then!"

The preparation for the upcoming trip was the most harrowing experience of Marta's life. The secrecy and planning was unlike anything she had ever done and with every item she stashed away, her sense of regret grew. Caleb had proposed to her hastily in his family's barn one night, only hearing of her desire to make the move through Frederick. He had wasted no time bombarding her with more fantastical plans which now fell on deaf ears before getting down on one knee and taking her hand. When she thought back on it, she could not remember what words he had spoken or if she had actually accepted his proposal. It was as if it was inherently understood that they were to be married.

"We'll do it when we get to California. Amish weddings are so dull," Marta did recall Caleb saying. It had made her sad. Amish weddings were always so beautiful to her, so filled with happiness and community. She could not imagine being wed in a small chapel without being surrounded by the friends and family she had known her whole life. *That's not true. Frederick will be there. He is your family and you are all the family he has now,* Marta reminded herself.

Oddly, Marta suddenly found that Noah came calling more frequently, almost as if he had sensed that something was amiss. She tried to distance herself from him but her resolve was weak and she continued to allow herself to be courted by him, even though she was betrothed. Of course, the engagement was still a secret so Noah had no reason to suspect anything but the shame growing within Marta was almost insurmountable. *This is unfair to Noah,* she told herself time and again but it did not stop her from spending her free time in his company. He truly was everything she wanted in a companion. He continued to send her flowers and share history lessons with her. Marta found herself envisioning what their children would look like and again would be overcome with guilt.

The weeks began to fly by and the hidden cache of clothing and goods to sell grew in the loose floorboard in the woodshed. On the Tuesday prior to the Friday of their scheduled departure, Marlin stumbled upon Marta's luggage. His gray eyes were filled with despair as he entered her room, carrying the sack filled with clothing.

"Marta, what is this?" he asked, sounding defeated. All the blood drained from her face as he entered the room and closed the door.

"*Daed*, it's not what you think!"

"Are you certain? It looks as if you are planning to leave, Marta. Are you leaving us too?"

She opened her mouth to respond and suddenly tears poured from her eyes and down her cheeks.

"I don't want to!" she confessed, throwing herself into her father's arms. "I want to stay here but I can't let Frederick go!"

Marlin Chandler stroked his daughter's long, chestnut hair and murmured comfortingly until her sobs lessened and she was slightly more coherent.

"Why do you have to go? Where is Frederick going?"

Marta sat up, tears slowing to a trickle and she stared at her father, begging him to understand.

"He wants to go to California with Caleb," she told him. Marlin's face scrunched in confusion.

"Caleb is going to California?" he asked, puzzled. "But Caleb is baptized. He will be ex-communicated." Miserably, Marta nodded.

"I have agreed to marry him and go with them both to California."

Marlin nodded, understanding lighting up his eyes but now his expression was clouded with concern.

"But you don't want to go?"

"No, *Daed,* I want to stay here. I don't even want to marry Caleb! I want to marry Noah!"

As the words left her lips, Marta flushed crimson. She should not have said so much, made such a display in front of her father. Even so, she felt very relieved that she had been able to tell someone what had been on her mind for so long. Marlin stood up, staring at his daughter pensively.

"Where are you going?" she asked, wiping her face, a concerned look crossing over her face.

"To find your mother."

"No! Oh *Daed,* no! Please don't tell her!"

Marlin leaned forward and gently caressed Marta's cheek.

"There is only one way to make this right, *liebchen*. And your mother is needed."

Marta's mouth dropped open in anguish as her father left the room. *What have I done?*

"Marta, Noah is calling!" Levi popped his head into the kitchen where she was stirring a stew. She continued to mix the thick soup, oblivious to her brother. It had been two days since her father had found the hidden cache of goodies and suspiciously, Marta had not seen him or Bridget since. Bridget had left word through Simon that Marta was to tend to the children until their return. In the meantime, the sense of distress Marta was feeling threatened to choke the life out of her. She had remained close to the house, terrified to visit either Caleb or Frederick, lest she had managed to get them in trouble.

"Marta!" She jumped this time as Levi pulled on her skirt. She looked down at his earnest brown eyes.

"Supper is almost ready, Levi. Just be patient!" she snapped. Immediately she regretted her tone as a hurt look appeared in his eyes.

"I'm not asking about supper. Noah is here," he repeated.

"Oh. Tell him I will call on him later," she lied.

"Tell him yourself. He's right there," Levi answered, pointing at the doorway. Marta spun and looked at the threshold. Noah stood with his hat in his hands at the entrance to the kitchen.

"I'm sorry to intrude," he said. "I can come back."

At the mere sight of him, Marta felt her resolve melt.

"No! Please come in. I didn't mean to sound rude. I am simply making supper. My parents have gone somewhere and I am to tend to the children until their return."

Noah nodded and ventured further into the room, glancing nervously at Levi.

"Go and get ready for supper, Levi. Leave us be." Levi scowled but obeyed, ducking out of the kitchen although Marta was sure he remained in earshot under the stairs.

"How are you, Marta?" Noah asked, sitting on the edge of a chair. "I feel as though you are putting a distance between us lately."

Without meeting his eyes, Marta busied herself with the stew, afraid that she would blurt out the truth if she stared into his beautiful face too long.

"Do you? I can't imagine why you feel that way," she lied.

"Can you look at me for a moment?" he pleaded. "I want to speak with you."

Reluctantly, Marta lowered the fire on the stove and turned to face him.

"Marta, I think you are wonderful," he told her, looking into her eyes. Uncomfortably, she shifted her gaze. "And until very recently, I thought that you liked me also."

Marta's eyes shot up.

"I do! I like you very much!" she told him.

"I have been feeling a slight rift between us but even so, I think we have many of the same dreams and values. What do you think?"

Marta nodded in agreement.

"I think that you and I would make a wonderful team. I would like very much if you would consider marrying me," Noah rushed on, shifting his own gaze, a pink hue touching his cheeks. Shocked, Marta, stepped back, a lump filling her throat. Tears stung her eyes and she began to shake her head.

"I...I can't," she whispered, her heart shattering with the words. Noah's face turned ashen as he looked up in disbelief.

"Wh-why not?" he choked.

The tears slipped down her cheeks and suddenly the world was spinning.

"Because I am already promised to someone else." Noah's face contorted in pain and his knees seemed to buckle beneath him.

"No!" Levi yelled. "No! You love Noah!"

"Levi, leave us be," Marta told her brother. "This does not concern you."

"Who?" Noah begged. "Who are you engaged to?"

"No one." Startled, Noah, Marta and Levi looked up at the door. Marlin and Bridget stood in the frame, smiling kindly at them.

"*Daed…*" Marta growled. "Please…"

She stopped speaking as Frederick stepped in from between his parents, his eyes shining with love.

"She is not betrothed to anyone," Frederick echoed. "Her fiancé has gone to California and he is not coming back."

"Freddy!" Levi screamed, throwing himself into his oldest brother's embrace. Frederick squeezed the boy back, grinning.

Marta's brow furrowed, not understanding.

"What do you mean?" she asked, quickly wiping away the tears from her face. She tentatively drew toward her older brother. He opened his arms and she ran in to hug him.

"*Mammi* and *Daed* came to me after *Daed* found your getaway bag. *Daed* told me what you told him, that you didn't want to marry Caleb and that you were only doing it for me, so I would have family."

Marta shot her father a look and he shrugged admittingly.

"I immediately went to see Caleb and told him that neither one of us were going, that we got cold feet and that he should go because Daed knew about his plan and was about to out him. So, he left last night, without a word to anyone. Not even you, apparently."

Marta didn't know whether to laugh or cry.

"But Frederick, you want to go to California," Marta said, feeling sick. Frederick drew her in for a hug.

"I thought I wanted to go to California, yes," he agreed. "But when I saw *Mamm* and *Daed* at the door to my little apartment, finally bonding together, worried about you, worried about me, I suddenly realized that I want my family more than I want anything else in this world. I would have never gone if you weren't coming with me, Marta. I've been a fool. I didn't realize how great I had it until I almost ruined your life. Thank you for always being there for me."

Choked with emotion, the Chandler family formed a group embrace until the sound of someone clearing their throat broke them apart. Noah stood uncomfortably, shifting from one foot to another.

"So...does this mean that you might consider giving me your hand in marriage, Marta?" he asked evasively. Marta burst into laughter and wriggled out of the arms of her family.

"Yes!" she replied, flinging her arms around Noah's neck.

ABIGAIL'S DILEMMA

SAMANTHA COLLIER

Abigail Esh watched as the familiar hills and plains of her small Pennsylvania community fell into view. It had been a long buggy ride; they had been travelling for half a day.

She felt a small stab of excitement, at the thought of finally coming home. She had been staying with some friends of her family, who were English, for the past month. It was all part of her *rumspringa*. She had sampled many things in the big city, including going to art galleries and English restaurants. It had been enjoyable, of course, and she wouldn't change the experience for the world.

But she wanted to return to her community, and start life as a fully committed adult Amish. She was ready.

At last. Her family's farmhouse was in view.

As the buggy pulled up, her eyes took in every detail: the old ramshackle farmhouse, the outbuildings and hen house. Home.

The front door opened, and her mother was down the veranda steps. Her eyes were shining in excitement.

"Abigail! We thought you'd never get here," she remarked.

Abigail stepped down from the buggy, embracing her mother. It felt like she hadn't seen her in years.

"Mammi! It is so good to be home," she said. "Where is everybody?"

Mrs Esh smiled, a bit indulgently. "Daughter of mine, have you forgotten the routine already?" They walked up the steps to the house, arm in arm. "Your father and brothers are in the fields, of course. They will return for lunch, as is always the way. Your sisters are quilting, over at Mrs Troyer's, as they do every Tuesday."

Abigail flung herself onto the living room sofa as soon as they entered. "It was such a long trip, Mammi. I feel black and blue all over."

"How are the Carlisles?" Mrs Esh walked to the kitchen as she spoke, getting the coffee she had just made and two cups.

"Very good." Abigail sat up, rubbing her eyes. "They send their best wishes. It was a bit of a whirlwind, staying with them."

"I could imagine." Mrs Esh poured the coffee. "Come, have your coffee. It will revitalise you."

Abigail did as her mother requested, walking to the table.

Suddenly, she stopped. She could see the figure of a man at the front door – tall, dressed in the traditional Amish clothing. He had taken his hat off.

Who was he? She had never seen him before. And her eyes seemed to be unaccustomed to the Amish dress. She had been so used to seeing English clothes that it stood out to her. Well, she would get used to it, again, of course.

"Mammi." Abigail gestured toward the door. "Someone is here."

Mrs Esh rose, approaching the door. "Oh, it is only Nicholas! He is helping your father and brothers; he has been here about two weeks, from another county." She opened the door. "Nicholas! What can I do for you?"

The young man smiled shyly, looking from Mrs Esh to Abigail. "I am sorry to disturb you, Mrs Esh. Your husband sent me to tell you not to prepare lunch today, as we are planning to work through."

"Work through?" Mrs Esh frowned. "Stay for a moment, Nicholas. I will prepare something quickly for you all to eat, which you can take back with you. You can't all work from dawn to sundown without food in your bellies. Please, come in and sit down while I get something ready."

Nicholas hesitated, then walked through the door.

"Abigail," Mrs Esh said, "Could you please pour Nicholas a coffee, while I get the food ready."

"Of course, Mammi," said Abigail, glancing sideways at the handsome, shy young man. Who was he? Why was he working here?

"I'm Abigail," she said. "Please, sit down."

The young man did as he was told. Abigail poured him a coffee, then sat down beside him.

"How did you come to work with us?" she asked, taking a sip of her own drink.

"I was looking for some short term work," Nicholas replied, blushing slightly. "I am on my *rumspringa*, and wanted to experience life outside my community for a bit. My father knows yours, from many years ago, and got in contact." He paused, staring at her. "I'm sorry, but you are Abigail, who has been on your own *rumspringa*?"

"*Ja*," Abigail agreed. "I have only just returned, after staying with some English friends in the city."

"Did you have a good time?"

"I did," Abigail said. She looked at his hands gripping the coffee cup. Strong, and firm. "But I am happy to be home. The city life is not for me. The Lord has made that very clear."

"I am glad," he said, smiling at her. He had the bluest of eyes, the colour of the sky on a bright summer's day.

Mrs Esh came back in, carrying a paper bag filled with sandwiches. She handed it to Nicholas.

"Please, finish your coffee," she said, as he stood up.

"Thank you Mrs Esh, but I must return to work," he said. "And thank you for the food. I am sure we will all appreciate it."

He smiled at Abigail, ducking his head. Then he left.

Abigail stared after him, sipping her coffee thoughtfully.

What a handsome young man. And such polite manners.

It was good to be home, for a lot of reasons. And it seemed that there was one more good reason, although Abigail hadn't realised when she had walked through the door.

The day was full of surprises.

***

Now that she was home, it seemed like she had never left. It was funny, how life worked in that way.

She had already been home a week, and was back into the old routine. And the most exciting thing of all was that Nicholas, the shy young man who was helping her family with the harvest, had asked her out on a date.

She didn't know where they were going, as she excitedly got herself ready on Saturday night. But she knew that Nicholas would take her somewhere appropriate, as well as fun. They had just clicked, right from the moment that she had laid eyes on him at the front door.

But he was shy. She had found many reasons to go and disturb her family as they worked, sometimes bringing snacks or drinks. Her brothers would grin at her – they knew what she was up to. She didn't usually come to visit them so often. It had worked. Eventually, Nicholas had asked her out.

Now they sat in Stoll's restaurant in town, having just finished a hearty meal and laughing over a coffee.

Abigail had never been able to speak so easily to a boy. It was like they couldn't keep up with everything they wanted to say to each other. She felt a glow within her, as she looked at him.

They were just thinking of leaving when the door to the restaurant opened. Abigail turned to look automatically. Then wished she hadn't.

Oh, no. It was Christian Raber. She swivelled quickly in her seat, staring straight ahead. Her heart had started to thump uncomfortably. Maybe, if she was lucky, he hadn't seen her.

But her luck wasn't in. She heard his footsteps behind, approaching their table.

"Abigail." He wasn't smiling. "I didn't know that you were back in town."

She turned and looked at him, a bit fearfully. "Just a week," she said, quickly.

Nicholas was looking from Abigail to Christian. He seemed perplexed.

"I am Christian Raber," the man said, extending a hand toward Nicholas. "Abigail has lost her manners, it seems."

Nicholas took the man's hand, shaking it. He looked at Abigail. "And I am Nicholas Fisher."

She stood up, quickly. "We were just leaving, Christian," she said, walking toward the door. Nicholas' eyes widened, but he stood up, too, almost forgetting his hat on the table as he followed her. He had to go back to get it.

They exited, into the cold night.

Christian stood for a moment, staring after them.

His eyes were cold.

***

"What was that all about?" Nicholas had to run to catch up to Abigail.

She turned, stopping to catch her breath. "I'm sorry," she said. "I know that I appeared rude. But I didn't want to speak to him. He has this idea that he is in love with me, and I have given him no encouragement. Honestly." She blinked back tears, staring up at him.

"What does he do?" Nicholas was frowning, staring down at her.

"Oh, nothing much," said Abigail. She was appalled to find that her hands were shaking. Stop it, she told herself. "He is always polite. He just doesn't seem to understand that I am not interested."

She paused, shaking her head slightly. "I have told him enough times. But he doesn't seem to understand. When I next see him, at Church or Evening Sing or wherever, he asks me out again, as if he hasn't listened at all."

Nicholas assisted her up into the buggy. "I am sorry, Abigail. It is hard when someone doesn't listen to you."

"*Ja*," she agreed. She tried to shake the image of Christian, in the restaurant, out of her mind. She was on a date, with Nicholas. Handsome, caring Nicholas.

"Don't worry about it," she said. "I am sure he will realise, eventually."

They rode off, into the night.

They didn't look back. If they had, they might have seen the figure of Christian, standing in the dark street, staring after the buggy long after it had disappeared.

***

"He was in Stoll's Restaurant, Mamm."

Abigail was having a hot cocoa with her mother after the date. Nicholas had dropped her off half an hour ago.

Mrs Esh frowned. "Don't read anything into it, Abigail," she said. "It might have been just co-incidence. Who knows, maybe he needed to get something from Stoll's."

"At nine-thirty on a Saturday night?" Abigail was frowning, too. "No, I know him of old. He followed me there, I am sure of it."

"He never threatens you, does he?" Her mother looked at her over the brim of the mug.

"No." Abigail shook her head. "He is always polite. It's just a feeling I get. He always seems to be where I go, and he won't stop asking me to date him. I think after the first three negatives, he might get the message that I am simply not interested in him in that way. But he never does."

Mrs Esh stood up. "Time for bed, I think. I will talk to your father about this. We don't want to offend the Raber's, but Christian needs to know that he can't harass you. We will have to think it through carefully, though."

Abigail nodded, bringing her mug to the kitchen sink.

"I almost forgot." Her mother looked at her. "How was the date with Nicholas? We got so caught up talking about Christian."

Abigail smiled broadly. "It was lovely," she beamed. "I think that I really like him, Mamm. Do you think he likes me, too?"

Mrs Esh smiled, her eyes softening as she looked at her lovely daughter. "How could he not, my *lieb*?" she replied. "But I don't know how long he is staying for, Abigail. Your father said that he only needed help for a few weeks, and they are almost up. He lives in the next county."

"That's not so far," said Abigail. "We could write letters."

"So you could," agreed her mother. "But it really is time for bed now, Abigail. We have Church tomorrow, don't forget. And I have to be up very early to cook the goose for the lunch."

Abigail followed her mother up the stairs, preparing for bed. She glanced down at her Bible, thinking whether she should look at it tonight or not. It was very late. But she was still feeling jittery after her encounter with Christian, and felt like she needed some comfort.

Her head was drooping over the good book when she suddenly jolted fully awake. What had disturbed her?

She took her candle, and got out of the bed, walking to her window. She peered out into the darkness, but she could see nothing. She tried to shake the feeling of unease away from her. She was being silly. She should blow out the candle, and climb back into bed.

And yet she stayed, staring out the window. It was complete darkness; not even the moon was out tonight, and a thick blanket of clouds had covered up the stars.

She dropped the curtain, and climbed back into bed.

But the unease didn't leave her. Instead, it invaded her dreams...

She was running.

In motion, she suddenly stopped. She looked down at her feet, willing them to move. But it was like they were frozen in quicksand; the more she tried to dislodge them, the firmer they set. She twisted and turned, in a frantic bid to free herself.

He was coming. She knew he was right behind her.

Suddenly, the quicksand turned to ice. She attempted to run, again. But her feet were sliding over the ice. She stumbled, trying to regain her balance.

She heard a noise behind her, and turned quickly.

It was him. She couldn't see him in the shadows, but she knew.

The ice started cracking underneath her feet. She watched it zig-zag, broken veins across the white surface.

And then she was gone, underneath the ice, plunged into cold, cold water.

She stared up, and saw him looking down at her, coldly...

She sat up in bed, breathing heavily. She could feel sweat sliding down her neck.

This had to stop. She didn't know what Christian's intentions were, but he had to know how much he was scaring her. She didn't think that he would harm her, not really. But he was behaving oddly, and she couldn't deny anymore that it was starting to affect her.

She lay back down, drifting back to sleep. Think happy thoughts, she told herself.

The image of Nicholas filled her mind. His handsome face, concerned for her that night when she had told him about Christian. The way that he had helped her down from the buggy when they had arrived home, holding her hand tenderly so that she wouldn't slip. She had looked into his eyes, and seen kindness. His eyes shone with the purity of his soul.

Nicholas. Was she falling in love with him? But she hardly knew him. It had only been their first date, and they had chatted a handful of times before.

And soon he would leave. Return to his farm in the next county, away from her. His *rumspringa* over, just like hers was.

Would she see him again?

The image of Nicholas was the last thing that she remembered as sleep finally claimed her – this time for the whole night.

***

Abigail yawned, trying to stifle it with her hand discreetly.

It was the next day, and she was tired. It had been late before she had finally drifted off to sleep. She looked around at the familiar faces at the church service, but she hadn't seen him yet.

Nicholas. Her heart leapt as she said his name in her head, over and over.

Where could he be?

She tried to concentrate on the service, but her mind was drifting. Her mother had told her that Nicholas had attended their church service since he had been staying with them. And he himself had said that he would see her there. He had been looking forward to her mother's baked goose with apple and cider gravy for lunch, as well.

She surreptitiously scanned the congregation, again. But then she saw Christian Raber, staring at her from the back row. Shivers coursed through her; her skin crawled like it had been invaded by an army of ants.

She looked to the front, trying to concentrate on the service.

But her eyes, sickeningly, were drawn back to him.

He hadn't stopped staring. But now he added a small smile.

She refused to smile back. It would just encourage him. Silly, she chided herself. Even turning her head to look at him again he would perceive as encouragement.

He had always been an intense boy, ever since they had shared a seat in the one room classroom down the road. She could remember that he often would be alone, kicking a stone in the playground while groups around him played. And when he had friends, it would always be only one person, or two. Usually children who were a bit odd, like himself.

She had never been anything but polite to him, but she had drawn the line at friendship. She just couldn't stomach his intense stares. How he had perceived her politeness as anything other than that was beyond her. And yet he had. He had been asking her out for over six months now.

At first, she had been flattered, despite herself. But then it had got annoying. He simply wouldn't listen to her, when she said no. And then he started turning up everywhere that she went: a visit to the bakery, or when she was perusing stalls at the market. Anywhere.

It was one of the reasons she had gone so far away for *rumspringa*. Abigail wasn't much of a traveller, really. She probably would have stayed closer to home. But she had needed a break from his constant attention.

The service finally finished, and people started socialising. She went up to her mother.

"Where is Nicholas?" she whispered. "I haven't seen him today."

Mrs Esh looked at her. "I'm sorry, I forgot to tell you, Abigail," she said. "Nicholas received a note this morning, about something urgent. He needed to return home immediately. I'm not sure if he will be back, my *lieb*. He was due to finish work soon with us, anyway." She looked at her daughter. "Cheer up! You can still write to each other."

Abigail felt her heart sink. She shouldn't be so disappointed, of course. They had only had one date, and Nicholas had a life of his own, far away.

But she *was* disappointed. She couldn't deny it.

She was staring at the wall of the barn, lost in her own thoughts. She didn't see Christian approach until it was too late.

"Abigail." He bowed, slightly. His cold eyes were assessing her, as always. She often felt he looked at her like something strange he had just discovered on the sole of his shoe.

"Christian, I'm sorry, but now is not a good time," she said, quickly. Why was he always silent when he approached her? If she had some warning, she could have scurried away.

"I hear that the young man you went on a date with last night has left us," he continued, as if she hadn't spoken at all. "Very suddenly. Did you know that Frannie Glick knows him and his family? She was just telling me that he has a fiancée, back home."

Abigail gasped. She shook her head. "No, Christian, I am sure that you are mistaken," she replied. "Nicholas didn't mention anything to me about a fiancée. He is an honourable man."

"Is he?" Christian smiled, coldly. "How well do you really know him, Abigail?"

She frowned. She supposed it was true, to a degree. She had only known Nicholas a week, after all.

But she trusted her instincts. He was a good man, she knew it. He wouldn't have deliberately deceived her about having a fiancée.

"Well, I shall talk to him," she said, turning away. "I really must go, Christian. I have to help my mother with the lunch."

She walked away quickly, ducking amongst people. Hopefully he wouldn't follow her.

Was it true? He had said he had got the information from Frannie Glick. She looked around, but couldn't see her.

She frowned. Oh, well. Frannie would turn up, sooner or later. And then she would ask her, how she had come by this information that Nicholas had a fiancée.

As Christian claimed.

She felt the skin crawling on the back of her neck. She looked around, and, of course, he was staring at her. An upsurge of anger shot through her. Would he ever leave her alone?

***

"He did mention a girl he had been dating..." Mrs Esh frowned, squinting her eyes, trying to remember. "Or was it that they had dated in the past? I'm sorry, Abigail. I simply don't remember. But he never mentioned a fiancée, of that I am sure."

Abigail frowned, too. It wasn't the simple yes or no answer that she was wanting. This was very frustrating.

She didn't have a right to demand an answer of Nicholas. They had made no promises to each other; it had only been one date, after all. But she also felt that he did owe her an answer, because it simply wasn't done to be dating someone behind his fiancée's back, if he had one.

If it was true, she never would have agreed to go out with him. It was as simple as that.

Restless, Abigail stood up. "Do you need me for anything else, Mamm? If not, I might go to my room, study my bible for a while."

Mrs Esh looked at her. "Of course, Abigail," she said. "Just come down to help with supper, that's all I require."

Abigail left, bounding up the stairs.

Mrs Esh watched her go, shaking her head slightly.

Her daughter was in a state, and had been since Nicholas had left so suddenly the day before. Mrs Esh was worried about her. It was unlike Abigail. And what was this business with Christian Raber? Abigail hadn't mentioned it to her until after her date with Nicholas. If it was true, it wasn't good, and they should intervene on her behalf. But what if Abigail was just being fanciful? The Rabers were good friends of theirs. Mrs Esh didn't want to cause conflict without reason.

She frowned, pondering. No, they would do nothing, for now. If Abigail continued to be worried, well, they would do something then.

She sighed. It was hard, being young. Navigating your way into adulthood. She might mention some bible passages that Abigail should study, to try to ease her mind.

***

Abigail finished the letter, signing her name at the bottom thoughtfully.

She had been in two minds about whether to write to Nicholas, but she was so wound up she didn't know what else to do. Even if she didn't send the letter, it had felt good to get her thoughts and feelings out onto paper.

She read back over what she had written. She had tried to not be too intense, but still convey her wish to continue corresponding with him. She hadn't mentioned anything about him having a fiancée, except to implicitly imply that if he was seeing someone where he lived, she would stop communicating with him.

She put the letter in an envelope, and sealed it. She wasn't sure of his address; she would have to ask her mother if she knew it.

She left it on her desk, propped up against her lantern.

It was time to help her mother with supper.

***

Outside the farmhouse, Christian could see Abigail leave her desk. He saw the letter. He could guess who it was to. And he knew how to solve this, as well.

He often watched her. He had found a position, quite hidden. He would come over the back way to the house, through the fields, being careful to avoid her father and her brothers working.

He didn't think that he was doing anything wrong. He had, after all, explained to her that he wanted to take her out. It was his intention to make her his wife. She was hesitant, and had said no, but that didn't unduly concern him. His father had told him that girls sometimes said no when they meant yes. His own mother, apparently, had refused his father a few times before finally agreeing to date him.

She just needed a little bit of persuasion, that was all.

He frowned, thinking of when he had walked into the restaurant and seen her on a date. It simply would not do. No other man was allowed to date his Abigail.

It had been a stroke of luck that Nicholas Fisher's father had suddenly needed him back at home; as soon as he had heard that, he seized the opportunity. Frannie Glick was away on her *rumspringa*, and couldn't contradict his story about a fiancée. Frannie was a friend of his, anyway, and as soon as she was back he would contact her and persuade her to corroborate the story.

He smiled. It was all going to plan. He had to get rid of Nicholas once and for all, discredit him in Abigail's eyes. And then he would be there, to pick up the pieces.

She would finally see that he was the one for her.

***

The letter had been sent. Abigail waited for a response, but none came.

Inside, she fretted a little. It was all so strange. She had thought that she and Nicholas had a real connection. But he wasn't responding to her – did that mean that what Christian said was true? That Nicholas had a fiancée back home, and that she had been a diversion while he was away?

But as the days went by, and no letter came, Abigail had to admit it to herself. Nicholas didn't care.

Oh, well. She went about her chores as normal, and smiled and laughed when she was required to. She let no one see her sorrow. It would get better, in time. Of course, it would. They had only known each other a short time. It wasn't as if it was a deep wound.

She studied her bible. The classic passage from Ecclesiastes 3:4, about there being a time for sorrow as well as joy, comforted her. She knew that life couldn't be good, all the time. You could learn from sorrow, and had to accept that sometimes there was sorrow in life. As surely as the tides ebb and flow on the shore, sorrow and joy would come and go.

So Abigail kept telling herself, as the days drifted into weeks.

***

The women sat around the table, picking up their needles to commence their quilting bee.

Abigail picked up hers with a sigh. It had been three weeks, and she had not received a word from Nicholas. It was time to let it go, put it behind her. They had connected, but he had decided that it wasn't worth pursuing. Or, he did have a fiancée at home, and he had been merely dallying with her. Abigail preferred to think it was the former; she didn't want her last impression to be that he was a dishonourable man.

They heard another buggy pulling up outside the farmhouse. The women looked at each other.

"Are we expecting someone else?" Mrs Esh turned to the women.

Frannie Glick walked through the door, puffing slightly.

"Frannie!" Mrs Mueller put down her needle. "We weren't expecting you! Aren't you supposed to be on your *rumspringa*?"

"*Ja*," answered Frannie, smiling at the group. "I returned yesterday, a few days early. Mammi told me that you were meeting today, and I wanted to catch up with you all."

Frannie took her seat, and started answering questions about her *rumspringa*. She had been staying with cousins in Ohio, and had a wonderful time.

Abigail glanced at her as she worked. She was waiting for the break, so she could ask her about Nicholas. It probably didn't matter, anymore. But she wanted to know.

At last, the women started getting up. One went to the kitchen, to prepare coffee and snacks. Frannie rose, and walked to the window.

"Frannie," Abigail said, walking up to her. "It is nice to have you back. I was just interested to know. Christian Raber was telling me that you know Nicholas Fisher and his family."

"Who?" Frannie looked at her, a puzzled expression on her face. "I don't know any Nicholas Fisher, Abigail. I think you must be mistaken."

"Are you sure?" Abigail frowned. "Christian told me that you knew the family, and that Nicholas had a fiancée back where he lives."

Frannie continued to look at her, bewildered. "I have no idea what you are talking about, Abigail. The only Nicholas I know is Nicholas King, who we went to school with."

"I'm sorry," Abigail said. "I must have misheard him. Thank you, anyway."

She turned around, and walked out of the house. She needed to be alone, for a moment. She needed to think.

She sat down on a seat on the porch, thinking deeply.

Frannie didn't know the Fishers. She had never heard of Nicholas. Which meant one thing: Christian had lied to her. About Frannie knowing them, but also about Nicholas having a fiancée.

She felt herself go cold. This was getting serious.

Christian had always been an annoyance. But now, he was actively interfering in her life.

She didn't know what to do. Just that it had to stop, once and for all. He had no right, and she was going to make sure that he knew it.

***

Abigail dressed carefully for the meeting.

She had spoken to Mrs Raber, asking her could she come over for a visit. There was something she needed to discuss with her and her husband, urgently. She also requested that Christian be there for the meeting.

She didn't tell her mother. She knew that she would be concerned about making waves with the Rabers. It was something she was concerned about, too. But she also knew that it couldn't continue. Christian had to be stopped. And the best way of ensuring that was to enlist his parents. Abigail knew Christian. He was obedient to his parents, and his father ruled him with an iron fist.

And it was something that she felt must do, by herself. She had to stand up for herself, once and for all.

Mrs Raber opened the door, and led her to the kitchen table. Coffee and cakes were there, waiting.

"Oh, you shouldn't have gone to so much trouble," Abigail said. She was sweating, a little, and her hands when she took the coffee cup were shaking. She wasn't looking forward to this.

Mr Raber was already there, looking at her expectantly. And then Christian came into the room.

He didn't look happy. But he sat down at the table. Obviously, his parents had insisted.

"So." Mrs Raber looked at Abigail, expectantly. "What did you need to see us about so urgently, Abigail?"

Abigail cleared her throat. She must be strong, but she was very nervous. It could backfire on her, and the Rabers might evict her from their home, saying that she was lying.

How should she proceed?

"Thank you for seeing me," she stated. "I know you are all busy people. I needed to see you about Christian."

Christian looked at her, his face like thunder. She almost balked, but doggedly continued.

"As you know, Christian and I have known each other a long time," she said. "Since school. I have always liked him as a friend, but lately, Christian has been wanting to court me."

Mr Raber smiled. "Nothing wrong with that."

"No," Abigail continued. "There isn't. But I have told Christian many times that I am not interested in him that way, and he continues to pester me. He doesn't listen to my wishes."

Mrs Raber looked at Christian, anxiously. "Is this true, Christian? Have you been pestering Abigail, when she has clearly said no?"

"She wants to go out with me," Christian blurted. "I know she does! She just needs persuading. Isn't that so, Daed? You always told me that women often don't know their own minds, and need a firm hand."

Mr Raber frowned. "That is not what I meant, Christian. Yes, sometimes a girl takes a bit of wooing. But if a young woman has clearly said no to you, repeatedly, then you must do the honourable thing and accept her decision."

"But...but..." Christian shook his head, colouring. "I know that she loves me, deep down!"

Abigail looked at him, coldly. "That is wrong, Christian," she said. "I don't love you, and never will. I have no desire to hurt you, but you must accept what I say. I don't want to court you. I like you just as a friend." That was a little white lie. She didn't like Christian, at all. But she didn't want to completely destroy his confidence in himself.

"Abigail, your wishes will be respected," said Mr Raber, glaring at his son. "I will make sure of it. Christian will not bother you anymore."

"Thank you," breathed Abigail. She turned to Christian.

"I wish you well, Christian," she said. "I hope that you find the woman that you will marry, one who loves you. But she is not me. I hope we can still be friends. Will you shake my hand?"

She offered her hand across the table to him. He looked at it as if he might refuse, then he grudgingly shook it. Mrs Raber looked relieved.

"I must go," said Abigail, rising. "Thank you all so much for letting me speak, and taking me seriously. It means the world to me."

"God speed, Abigail," Mrs Raber replied. Mr Raber smiled at her.

It was over. Christian would not bother her, again. She knew the Rabers, and that they demanded complete obedience. Christian would not dare to defy them, now that they knew. She would have preferred that he realised by himself, but that might never happen.

She had to protect her life. He had already interfered in her budding relationship with Nicholas. She didn't want him to interfere for a minute longer.

***

Abigail was feeding the hens when a shadow fell across her.

Fear gripped her. Oh, no. It wasn't Christian back – was it?

She looked around. Then gasped. It wasn't Christian who stood there, but another tall man.

It was Nicholas!

She stood up, slowly. She couldn't quite believe that he was here.

He smiled at her, a bit tentatively. "Abigail," he said. "Your mother said that you would be here."

"Here I am," she replied, then could have kicked herself. Couldn't she think of anything better to say?

"Do you want to go inside?" He asked. "I need to talk to you."

She nodded, leading the way out of the hen house.

They sat at the kitchen table, staring awkwardly at each other.

"I thought..."

"I'm sorry..."

They laughed, as they realised they had both spoken at the same time.

"You go," said Nicholas, looking at her as if he had never seen her before in his life. It made her glow.

"I thought that you didn't want to see me again," Abigail said, biting her lip.

"I thought the same," Nicholas replied. "When you didn't answer my letter."

"What letter?" Abigail frowned. "I never received a letter from you. I wrote *you* a letter, which you never replied to!"

Nicholas shook his head, frowning. "I don't understand. I never received a letter from you. But I did send one."

Abigail stared at him, perplexed. Then understanding started to dawn on her face.

"It must have been Christian," she said. "I didn't realise he was going to that level. He must have been monitoring our mail box. Mamm leaves letters we want to send in there for Daed to collect and send when he gets to town."

"Christian?" Nicholas frowned. "That man who has been pestering you?" He paled, and stood up. "This is going too far. I will go around to his house, this minute!"

"Nicholas, sit down," Abigail said. "It's alright. I have spoken to his parents. He won't be bothering me anymore."

"Are you sure?" Nicholas sat down, slowly. "Because if he ever tries again, he will have me to answer to!" Abigail could see a vein throbbing in his temple. He was angry.

"So you care about me?" She looked at him, shyly.

"I do," he replied. "So much so, Abigail, that I travelled here today to speak to you, even though I thought you didn't answer my letter." He paused, looking like he didn't know what to say further.

"I care for you, too, Nicholas," she said, shyly. "Can we begin again? Like before Christian started interfering in our lives. He told me you had a fiancée, back home."

"He what?" Nicholas looked gobsmacked. "That is an outright lie! I would never have asked you out on a date if I had a fiancée. You didn't believe it, did you?"

"I tried not to," Abigail answered. "But when you didn't reply to my letter, I thought the worst. It was Christian, all along."

"We can begin again," Nicholas said, looking at her earnestly. "If you are willing?" He reached for her hand, across the table. "And God willing, of course."

"Nothing would please me more," Abigail replied. She took his hand. Happiness swelled up within her.

Christian was out of their lives. Nicholas cared for her.

The time for joy was upon them.

THE END

MY HEART GOT LOST

DEIDRA SCOTT

DEIDRA SCOTT

Chapter One

Rows of black buggies and waiting horses were parked around the small white farm house. In the front yard, little boys ran through the grass, chasing one another across the damp April ground.

John Yoder watched the children from his kitchen window. Occasionally, a fellow-Amish man would walk behind him and give him a pat on the back. Their gentle words of comfort did nothing to ease the pain in John's heart.

"Sarah is in a better place now," one of the men told him before they said their goodbyes.

Yes, Sarah was in a better place now. John knew that. After six months of watching his wife wither away, her body slowly consumed by the fast-spreading cancer, he knew that she was finally at peace. Caring for her as she writhed in pain had done more to age John than he wanted to admit.

"Good things are coming," an Amish woman tried to assure him as she gathered her children to leave.

That morning they had finally put Sarah in the soft spring ground. Her body would rest in the Amish cemetery now – her spirit finally free from all she had endured.

One by one the other Amish gathered their families and left John's home. And as night closed in, he found himself all alone.

John made his way to the kitchen where he sat down at the table with a cold cup of coffee.

He and Sarah would have been married for twenty years that spring. He took a sip of his coffee. In all that time, John had held a secret in his heart. A secret he hoped that Sarah had never discovered.

A knock on the front door brought John to his feet.

"Who could that be?" he wondered aloud. At eight-thirty, he was certain it was too late for any of the other Amish to be calling.

When John opened the door, he couldn't help but take a deep breath. On the front porch stood a young man he could hardly recognize.

"*Daed*," the voice of the stranger sounded familiar, "I've come home, *Daed*."

Even though he was sporting a pair of blue jeans and a tee-shirt, it certainly was John's only son.

"Sam..."John didn't think he could find the right words to say. He opened the door wider and waited on his son to come inside.

"I heard about Mom," Sam muttered softly, "I am so sorry..."

John reached out an arm and put it on his son's shoulder, "Have you been doing okay, out there in the *Englisher* world?"

Sam took a deep breath, "I'm sorry I left, *Daed*. It wasn't fair to leave you here alone. I just couldn't stand to watch her suffer like that."

John knew that his son spoke the truth. Although Sam had always been a bit of a rebel, it was his mother's sickness that finally drove him away from the Amish community.

"I needed to get away."

John nodded slowly, "*Jah*, I understand."

"I'm not home for good." Sam whispered softly, "I'm only here to see you. I needed a fresh start, *Daed,* and I think I've found one. Maybe you could use a fresh start too?"

John opened his eyes in surprise. Leave the community? Leave the faith? Was his son serious?

"I couldn't...." John started, but then stopped short. He'd already fooled enough people. He'd been playing the part of a liar for twenty years. Maybe it was time for something new.

He took a deep breath and started again, "When do we leave?"

Chapter Two

Leaving behind everything had been difficult for John. He didn't tell anyone that he was going. He simply got in his son's shiny new car the next morning and left. Something about leaving behind his farmhouse felt good. John wouldn't miss it.

Sam lived in a nice apartment and had a job working at a factory making tires for cars.

John knew that he had to do some kind of work or he would drive himself crazy simply sitting in his son's empty apartment. Sam had a quick answer to his job dilemma.

"You could be a driver!" Sam suggested, "Just like we used to hire drivers when we were in the Amish community; many people in the city don't have their own vehicles and need someone to get them to work or appointments."

"I could never drive," John scoffed, "A buggy perhaps but not a car!"

Despite John's uncertainty, his son was persistent. Sam was determined that his father would learn how to drive and that he would get a job providing others with transportation.

When Sam wasn't working at the factory, he would help his dad learn how to drive.

While the city life helped to keep John distracted somewhat, nights were still long and difficult. He had a hard time sleeping; instead, he would stare at the ceiling, thinking about Sarah and wishing that he could have been a better husband to her.

Sarah had been so sweet, so kind, and so gentle to him.

But John had never loved her.

Not really.

In his heart, he reserved that love for a girl he had lost many years ago.

Becky.

Even thinking about her name still brought tears to his eyes. John had spent the last twenty-one years missing her. Every day, he had awoken and wished that she was the one by his side.

Poor Sarah had deserved better. But try as he might, Becky had always been on his mind and in his heart.

Sometimes he still found himself wishing that he could understand why she had left him. One day, they had been so close – and then she had faded out of his life. Their summer sunshine had quickly turned winter cold.

As John wiped tears from his eyes, he wished that he could start his entire life over. Maybe that's what the city would do for him. Maybe it truly could be a fresh start. Maybe he could put the ghosts of the past away once and for all.

Chapter Three

After living in the city for three months, John Yoder had seen his life change in so many ways. At Sam's persistence, he had done away with his Amish clothes and traded them in for a pair of jeans and a button-up shirt. His beard had been shaved away and his hair cut more like an *Englisher*.

But, no matter what John did to try to escape his past, it felt like he was constantly haunted by the ghosts of what could have been and what should have happened.

With a little practice, John soon got his driver's license and was able to get around the city with ease. Using a minivan, he advertised his services and made a lot of money taking people from place to place. It was so strange to be the one driving rather than the passenger!

"I wonder what is happening back home?" John thought to himself as he pulled up to a small apartment and waited on his passenger to come out.

He never knew who he was likely to pick up. Sometimes he drove teenagers to the mall, other times impoverished mothers and their children to doctor appointments, and other times he ended up taking drunken people home from parties.

John tapped his fingers on the steering wheel as he waited on his next client.

It had been three months to the day since Sarah had passed. Each day, John was constantly overwhelmed by the guilt of what he had done.

The sliding door opened before John even realized that his passenger had arrived.

"I need to go to the supermarket," a woman's voice spoke up softly with directions.

Something about her voice...John could hardly believe his ears. He was almost too afraid to even turn around and look, but forced himself to glance in the rear view mirror.

Sitting in the backseat of his blue minivan was a petite brown-haired woman who appeared to be in her mid-thirties. She was dressed in Amish clothing and was busy fumbling for something in her black bag.

Becky.

It had to be her. Even after all these years, she still looked the same.

John felt as if his heart would beat out of his chest. Grabbing for his sunglasses, he scrambled to put them on and cover more of his face than what was already hidden beneath his ball cap.

Could it really be her? John would almost swear that it was, but started to wonder if the stress of life was simply getting to him. Perhaps his troubled mind had begun to play tricks on him.

As he turned the van onto the highway, John announced, "I don't see many Amish people in this town."

His passenger gently laughed and said, "I suppose not. I'm probably the only one. Not many Amish live in towns."

"What brought you here?"

John knew that he had over-stepped his bounds. This woman, be it Becky or not, didn't know him from Adam. No Amish woman would want to tell all her personal stories to a man she hardly knew.

She was silent for a moment and then announced, "I haven't always lived in the city. But things change."

"I used to live near some Amish out in the country." John revealed, hoping to catch some sort of information that would tell him if this truly was his Becky from so long ago.

"Hmmm..." was all that she said.

The ride to the grocery store was very quiet, but John felt as if his heart was beating loud enough to hear it. He wanted so desperately to say something, to ask this woman her name, to discover if she truly was the woman he had loved with all his heart, but didn't know where to start.

As he waited for her to get out of the grocery store, John tapped his finger restlessly on the steering wheel, wondering what he should say.

"Well, I'm ready to go home," the Amish woman announced as she opened the van door and loaded up her few bags of groceries.

John started the engine and waited for her to settle back in the seat.

"No where else?" He asked, hoping that another stop would give him a chance to say something to her.

"No. Just home."

John glanced back in the rear view mirror, watching her as he pulled out of the parking lot. The ride home was just as quiet as the trip to the store.

When he pulled up to the apartment building, John swallowed hard, searching for something to say.

Before he could open his mouth, she asked, "Could you possible take me to the chiropractor in the morning?"

John didn't have to look at his schedule. He already knew the answer.

"Sure," he said, "What time?"

"Eight-thirty?" She asked.

John nodded his head and she gave a slight smile, "Then I'll see you tomorrow." She got out of the van and started to close the door before announcing, "Just so you'll know, my name is Becky."

Chapter Four

John couldn't believe that he had found her once again. He had been certain that Becky would be out of his life forever. He had only prayed for such a chance to come again.

But with the joy of his new discovery came the sickening reality that there was no hope for the future. Becky had left him before and, no matter how much time had passed, there was no reason that she wouldn't leave him again.

With Becky's memory came plenty of good thoughts but also terrible, deep pain. Just the realization of how much he had missed her brought on a new round of guilt. Poor Sarah. He had tried to be such a good husband to her but felt as if he had failed. He had never loved her the same way that he had loved Becky.

The next morning he picked Becky up for her appointment and wondered if he should tell her that he would be too busy to ever drive her again but, try as he might, he couldn't get the words to come out of his mouth.

"So," she settled back in the van seat after giving him directions to her chiropractor, "Tell me about yourself. I don't even know your name."

"It's..." John took a deep breath, "Jay."

"What is your life like, Mr. Jay?"

It was strange to think of Becky being so bold with a total stranger...especially someone she thought was an *Englisher*.

"I live with my son," he started awkwardly, "He has a little apartment on the edge of town. He works in a factory and I drive people."

John watched her nod in the rear view mirror.

"Do you have any children?" he ventured to ask.

Becky smiled sadly and shook her head, "No. I have no children. I have never been married."

Something about those words brought a lump to John's throat. He was happy to know that his true love had not given her affection to another and yet, knowing that she had left him for someone else would have been better than simply having her leave for no reason at all.

"Where is your wife?" She suddenly asked.

John took a deep breath, "She died...it's been three months. She had cancer for a long time. She battled it off and on all her life, but this time the cancer won the battle."

"I am so sorry," Becky whispered. Her voice sounded so genuine. So like John remembered from long ago. It felt like you could hear her heart pouring out in her words, "Sorry that you had to go through that. Losing someone dear to you can be hard. I know that for a fact."

John was surprised to realize that they had already reached the chiropractor's office. The ride had been so pleasant; he could hardly believe how fast the time had passed.

The wait seemed like it took hours, but Becky came out with a smile on her face.

"Anywhere else?" John asked.

When Becky shook her head no, John took a bold move, "Would you mind if I stop for a cup of coffee and a donut?"

"Of course not!" She assured him.

John pulled into a small donut shop and hurried inside. He went up to the counter and ordered two strawberry donuts and two cups of coffee.

"Oh," Becky exclaimed as he handed her one of the coffees and a donut, "You shouldn't have done that!"

"It's my treat."

"You made a good choice," she announced as she took a bite of the gooey treat, "Strawberry is my favorite. I used to make them all the time."

John could remember the picnics that they had together by the river. Becky had always brought a batch of her homemade donuts. Somehow the one he was eating tasted bland in comparison to the wonderful-good memory.

When John took Becky to her apartment, she pulled out her checkbook and asked, "How much for the ride?"

"No charge." He announced.

"You can't work for nothing," she started to protest but he stopped her.

"I got a donut and some coffee. That was plenty."

Becky smiled and cocked her head to the side, "Thanks then. I'll get back with you."

John watched as she stepped out of the van and started toward her apartment. She had said nothing else about another ride. Was this to be the last time he would see her?

"Please, God," he prayed softly, "Let me see this dear woman again!"

Her smile hadn't changed. It had been twenty-one years since he last saw it and it felt like a step back in time. A little lopsided, but beautiful.

As he drove back to his son's apartment, John remembered the day that he first saw that smile. He had been eighteen years old. John had been dating Sarah for two years and he was thinking about asking her to be his wife. That summer Sarah had left to go stay with her aunt in Indiana, leaving John completely alone. One of the Amish families was hosting a gathering for the young people and Becky had been there visiting from a nearby community.

Becky was sixteen-years-old with curly dark hair and a sparkle in her eyes. When she first looked at John and smiled, he was instantly smitten. Suddenly, all thoughts of Sarah were gone as he fell madly in love with this younger girl.

He had sent Sarah a letter, explaining that it was time for them to take a break from their relationship and had then pursued Becky. They had great times together. He could remember sitting outside of the young peoples' meetings on his buggy, so full of things to say to each other that they couldn't force themselves to go inside and enjoy the fun. They had counted stars together, made wishes together, and dreamed of the future.

Then summer had come to an end. And, as quickly as she had appeared, Becky was gone. John had sent her one letter after another but she never replied. He had even gone to her house but she wouldn't come to the door.

When Becky was gone, Sarah reappeared. Sarah was familiar and stable. She was there to distract him from Becky. And, once John realized that Becky would never come back, he was ready to take the step forward and not only renewed their relationship but asked Sarah to marry him.

Even though Sarah became John's wife, he never loved her. Not like he had loved Becky.

Chapter Five

The next four days were difficult. All John could do was think about Becky. It felt that he had lost her once again. The pain was almost too much to bear. His mind was filled with her memories and, with those memories came a flood of guilt and confusion.

John would never understand why Becky had left him all those years ago. Had he done something wrong? Had she never truly loved him at all? Had he simply been used by a girl who wanted a beau for the summer?

And, worse yet, came the reality that he even cared. After all that had happened, he should have forgotten all about his old sweetheart. After twenty years of marriage, he should be mourning the loss of his wife.

John was sitting at the kitchen table, reading the newspaper when his phone began to ring.

"Hello," he answered the call from an unknown number.

"Hello Mr. Jay. It's Becky."

He didn't even have to hear her name to know who it was. John's heart skipped a beat and he found himself standing up in surprise, "Yes?"

"How are you?" She asked somewhat awkwardly.

"Oh, I'm doing well. Just waiting on my son to get home from work. Do you need to go somewhere?"

"No, I don't need a ride."

When he realized that he would not be able to see her, John felt a lump rise in his throat.

Before he could say anything else, Becky jumped ahead, "If you're not busy, would you like to come by for supper? It would make me feel good to repay you for the ride you gave me the other day."

John could hardly believe his ears. Becky was inviting him over for supper?

"What time?" He asked quickly.

"The food will be ready at five, but you can come earlier if you want."

"I'll be there!" John exclaimed. Hanging up the phone, John glanced at his watch and started preparing for the evening ahead.

He arrived at Becky's apartment at four-thirty.

Initially, things seemed cold and formal but, before long, they were laughing together. As strange as the situation seemed, it felt like John had gone back in time. Although Becky had aged over the last twenty-one years, she was still the same carefree girl who had stolen John's heart.

John helped her to prepare the meal and they laughed together when she left the rolls in the oven for too long and burnt them.

"Delicious," John announced as he took a bit of the pork roast and washed it down with some homemade lemonade.

"I learned from my mom," Becky announced with a smile.

"Is your family okay with you living here...alone...away from the community?" John asked suddenly, surprised that Becky was staying in an apartment by herself with electricity and other things from the *Englisher* world.

Becky shook her head sadly, "No. They are not happy at all. But they have grown used to it." She reached out and began clearing away some of the empty dishes, "I've been here alone for the past fifteen years."

John wanted to ask so many questions but all he could get out was, "Why?"

"You know, Mr. Jay," Becky took a deep breath and then started her story, "I am not married, but it's not because I don't want to be."

"You have a boyfriend?" John quickly asked.

Becky smiled tiredly and said, "No. Nothing like that. I had a beau once. I thought we would get married, really. I met him at a young peoples' meeting for the Amish and we spent the whole night talking. I felt as if I had met my soul-mate and, the more time we were together, the more certain I became."

Her voice trailed off and John found himself struggling to maintain his composure.

"Mr. Jay," she sighed sadly, "I loved that boy. I loved my John so deeply. I would not have given him up for anyone else." She shook her head and looked down at her hands.

"What happened?" John choked out the words.

"He already had a girlfriend," Becky whispered, "Her name was Sarah and she was one of my distant cousins. When he broke up with her to court me, I didn't realize how deeply it would hurt her. She was in a different state for the summer. In my mind, I thought she surely didn't love John as much as I. At least, I felt that way until she came to visit me. She look horrible, Mr. Jay. Her eyes were swollen and her face hollow. She was always a sickly girl. She told me that John had loved her and that her heart was broken."

At this point, tears were flowing down Becky's face as she finished her story, "I couldn't do it to her. I couldn't take away this girl's entire world. So, I left. I went back home and I never spoke to John again. For a while, he sent me letters. I burnt them. It hurt me too much to think of reading his dear writings. He came to see me but I wouldn't accept him. I stayed away from him. I knew that, if I was to see his face again, it would break my heart. I loved him so much. That's why I left my Amish community. My family wanted me to marry someone else, but I couldn't. That's why I'm here at this apartment. I would rather live alone than live with someone else."

"All these years," Becky's voice was now no more than a whisper, "I have wanted to tell John the truth. I want him to know how much he means to me. I have wanted to let him know why I left."

John opened his mouth to say something. He wanted to reach out and pull Becky to him, but was stopped short by the ringing of his cell phone. John almost ignored it until he saw that it was his son.

"Sam?" He asked, surprised to see that his son had called him.

"Dad," the voice on the other end of the line was shaky, "I'm at the emergency room."

Suddenly, all his thoughts were on his son. John left Becky alone with a sad smile and a quick explanation, and then hurried away to the hospital to see what had happened to his son.

Chapter Six

"I didn't mean for you to rush over to get me," Sam laughed as John stood over his son's bed in the emergency room, "I just need someone to take me home. I don't even think I need to be here...I would have kept working but the boss insisted I get checked out."

"What happened?"

Sam smiled and shook his head before wincing, "Oh, I just tripped and hit my head really good on a piece of machinery."

John breathed a sigh of relief and sat down in the chair next to the hospital bed. This day had been almost too much for John to handle. He covered his face with his hands. He had been so afraid that he was going to lose his son. Now, he was overwhelmed with emotion. He was so thankful that Sam was going to be okay, but found himself forced to focus on his visit with Becky.

He now knew the truth. Becky hadn't stopped loving him. She had given him up out of love for him. She had cared for Sarah and wanted to make sure she had a happy life.

What now?

John was almost thankful that Sam had called him away from the uncertain situation. He wasn't sure what he would have done or said if his phone hadn't interrupted his visit with Becky.

"Where were you anyway?" Sam asked as he reached up to gingerly pat his injured head, "I would have sworn I heard a woman talking in the background. Were you watching television?"

Sam should have known that his dad had little use for the television that was in his apartment. John shook his head 'no" and muttered, "It was just a friend."

"A friend?" Sam repeated in surprise, "Dad, I didn't know that you had friends...let alone lady friends. Obviously I need to spend a little less time at work and a little more keeping up with my *daed*!"

John rolled his eyes and tried to act unconcerned; however, he felt completely awkward and ill-at-ease.

"So, who was she?" Sam teased with a smile.

"No one." John answered sharply, "No one at all. Just an old friend."

Sam lifted his eyebrows and then winced when the movement made his head hurt.

"Dad...what's this about? Are you seriously seeing a woman?"

"Don't talk that way," John started, "Your mom just in the grave..."

"Dad," Sam's voice was serious now and he looked John straight in the eyes, "You took *gut* care of mom. You always provided for her and me, and you gave us a good life. But I could tell things were never right..."

John lowered his eyes in shame. All these years he had tried so hard to put on a good show and make everyone think he had felt more for Sarah than he truly had.

"Don't be ashamed," Sam assured him, "I can understand. You were faithful and good to us for all those years. But Mom's gone now. Your time with her is over...maybe it's time for you to really be with someone who makes you happy."

The voice of the doctor interrupted them as he pulled back the curtain and stepped into the room. Once again, John was saved an awkward conversation but he felt somehow disappointed. He felt as if he needed to talk to someone and his son's words made him feel better about all his choices throughout the years.

Just as Sam had predicted, there was nothing wrong with him. He had a goose egg on his head, but no serious damage. The doctor released him from the hospital and John drove him home in his van.

Once they were back at Sam's apartment, he sat down to watch some television while John fixed a frozen pizza that he found in the freezer.

"Thanks," Sam announced as he reached for the pizza his dad offered him.

"Sam," John sat down across from him and took a deep breath. He was so overcome by uncertainties that he needed to talk to someone.

Sam turned off the TV and gave his dad his full attention.

"Sam," John started again, "When I came to town with you, I was hoping to get away from all my mistakes. I have made many mistakes. Just like you said, I never had deep feelings for your mother. I spent my entire life pining away after a girl who left me when I was eighteen years old. Her name was Becky and I loved her all these years. Imagine how surprised I was when I found her right in this very town. Sam, I've been trying to get over her memory and forgive myself for not treating your mother better, but now I'm not sure what to do."

Sam's eyes were huge. In a moment, all his questions had been answered and he finally understood his father.

"Does she still love you?" He asked in surprise.

"She still loves John Yoder. She doesn't know that I'm him. She thinks I'm a man simply named 'Jay'. I wanted to tell her the truth, but I couldn't."

Sam started blankly as if he couldn't believe his own ears, "Dad, you have to tell her the truth. She deserves to know. You've both been mooning around over each other all these years...you and she both deserve some kind of closure."

John shook his head slowly, "I wouldn't even know where to start..."

"*Daed*," Sam reached out and patted his father's arm, "Just tell her the truth. Tell her what's in your heart."

Chapter Seven

John had never been as nervous in his life. He stood on the apartment porch, shifting from one foot to the other as he tried to gather enough courage to knock on the door. Slowly, he lifted a knotted fist and gave a sturdy rap against the wooden frame.

What would Becky say when she found out the truth? Would she be angry at him for hiding who he truly was? Would she be disenchanted to see the man that he had become?

Obviously she wasn't coming to the door. Perhaps she had left. Evening was starting to close in; maybe she had gone to bed.

John let out a sigh of mixed relief and disappointment, and started to turn. Suddenly, the door swung open and Becky was standing in front of him. She looked at him in surprise, her head cocked slightly to the side.

"You're back." She announced.

"Yes, I'm back."

"I was afraid that you were gone for good. How is your son?"

"He's fine." John took a deep breath, "Can I come inside?"

Becky stepped back and motioned for him to come into her apartment. She led him to a recliner and sat down on the couch next to him.

"I have something I need to tell you," John began awkwardly.

Becky looked at him expectantly, but he couldn't force the words to come.

"Yes?" She tried to nudge him along.

"Tonight, you told me a story about your old boyfriend..." John started only to stop himself and begin again, "I haven't always lived here. I've not always been a driver..."

He stopped and looked at Becky. She sat so close to the edge of the couch, he could reach out and touch her if he was bold enough. She stared at him, her dark eyes wide and questioning.

John couldn't handle it any longer, "I don't know how to begin to tell you this, but Becky...I am John Yoder."

The silence in the room was almost deafening. Becky opened her mouth and then shut it. John tried to read her expression, but he couldn't see past the tears that were forming in his eyes.

She took a deep breath, her chest rising and falling, as she gathered her composure.

"I shouldn't have come," John announced as he grabbed the chair arm and started to push himself up, "I am so sorry. I shouldn't have said a thing."

In an instant, Becky reached out a hand and put it on his, urging him to stay seated.

John relaxed back in his seat, surprised at her gesture.

She leaned forward in her seat and reached out to cup his face in her hand, "Oh, John," she whispered. The tenderness in her voice revealed twenty years of pain that had been waiting for a release, "Don't you realize that I've known it all along?"

John could feel his eyebrows rise in shock. Becky had known who he was the entire time? How was it possible?

Becky pulled her hands back and began to clasp them together on her lap, "Someone told me about a driver named John Yoder. I wasn't sure that it was you, but I had to call and see. John, I have waited so long to see you again. After what I told you today, I was so afraid that you wouldn't come back. I was afraid that you didn't care for me anymore. I was afraid that you would be angry or disgusted or..." Her soft voice trailed off and her words were replaced by her soft sobs.

Before he knew what he was doing, John was by her side on the couch. He reached out and enveloped her in his strong arms, pulling her close to him. He couldn't believe that this moment was real.

The past twenty years felt as if they had never happened as Becky returned his embrace. He leaned his chin against her shoulder, soaking in the smell of her lavender soap.

"Becky," He whispered her name over and over, "Dear, sweet Becky. I think I love you more now than ever."

"Then you don't hate me?" She sobbed, "After I left you, I thought you would hate me."

"I could never hate you!" John exclaimed, "You were nothing but a girl trying to do what was best for those you loved. I am only angry at myself for not caring more for Sarah. She was a good wife and you sacrificed yourself to make sure that she was happy."

Becky reached up to wiped her eyes, "Wait just a minute. I have to get something to show you."

John didn't want to let her go. He wanted to hold her in his arms forever, but he released her long enough for her to run into a back room and hurry back, a piece of paper in her hand.

"John, you need to read this."

With trembling hands, John took the piece of paper and began to read to himself.

"Dearest Becky,

I don't know how to start this letter to you. It has been twenty years since we last spoke. I still remember begging you to break things off with John so that he would marry me...it seems a lifetime ago.

I have had a good life Becky. The Lord blessed us with a beautiful son named Sam. He is now nineteen years old and has left the Amish faith. I continue to pray that he will leave the *Englisher* world and return home in good time.

As you know, I have always been sick. I am now in the end stages of cancer. There is no cure and I am slowly fading away.

John has been a blessing to me. No one could ever ask for a dearer, sweeter man. He spends every day by my side, and never lets me want for anything. No matter how tired he maybe, he is always ready to do what I need. I could not have ordered a better man.

I know that John still loves you. Every day, I can see the emptiness in his eyes. His heart has never been complete since you left him. And somehow, that makes his care for me even more precious. Even though I am not his soul-mate, he cares for me with his whole heart – which is an entirely different sort of priceless love. He may not love me as passionately as you, but I believe that he loves me as much simply in another way.

After twenty years of marriage, I find that it is now my turn to leave John. And, after years of my own selfish happiness, I want to give him back to you. Please, find him. Please, marry him. Make yourselves a happy life together.

With all my love,

Sarah"

John read the letter over and over again. Somehow, as he let those words sink into his heart, all of his guilt, pain, and resentment melted away.

It was true, he had loved Sarah; maybe not in the same romantic, passionate way that he loved Becky, but he had loved his wife. He knew that he could now forgive himself and move forward with his life.

"I have prayed so hard to find you, John." Becky whispered as she leaned her head against his shoulder.

John put his arm around her, pulling her tightly against his body.

"Becky," he choked out softly, "Will you be my wife? After all these years, will you still have me?"

Becky nodded her head, "Of course, John. That is what I want with my whole heart."

John lifted her chin with his thumb and tilted his head to the side. Leaning forward, his lips met hers. This was to be the first of many, many kisses to come.

Epilogue

John Yoder watched the children playing from his kitchen window. Rows of black buggies were parked in front of his house as groups of Amish families made their way toward the door. They were preparing for a work frolic to help John raise a new barn.

"What are you doing?" A soft voice whispered near his ear as Becky stepped up and put her arm around his waist.

"Just thinking, my love," he turned and pulled her closer to him.

So much had happened since that day a year ago when he had visited Becky in her apartment. Together they had returned to the Amish and were married together beneath the old oak tree in the front yard.

"There comes Sam," John announced with a smile as his son's black car pulled up into the driveway. Although Sam had yet to rejoin the Amish church, he came to frequently visit and help his father. John held out hope that Sam would eventually return to the faith and they could live their lives side-by-side.

"You'd better get out there and start to work," Becky stepped back, "I need to go check on baby Johnny."

John watched as his wife went to check on their newborn baby.

He had hoped for a fresh start after Sarah's death. His wish had been granted.

John smiled softly to himself. Life truly was good.

END

MEET ME BY THE POND

112

ABIGAIL THOMAS

Annabelle pinned the freshly cleaned linens to the line as she watched her twin daughters playing out in the yard with their cornhusk dolls. They had seen little Mary's beautiful porcelain doll that her wealthy grandmother in the city sent her and wanted ones of their own. She didn't enjoy having to explain to them that they couldn't afford such a nice doll, but once they got to make their own dolls out of cornhusks and twine they didn't seem to be bothered. Seeing them smiling and laughing outside in the sun was a breath of fresh air for Annabelle. She was grateful to have such hearty and happy children, especially after what happened to their father.

She shook off that heavy memory and continued hanging the laundry out to dry. There would be time to dwell on the past after the chores were finished. There was plenty to be done today, but not nearly as much as if she were running the ranch on her own. After the accident, Annabelle tried to the small homestead that she and her husband built together, but wasn't able to keep up with only the help of her two, grieving daughters. It wasn't long before Papa insisted that they sell the place and come to live with him back on the family ranch. Annabelle was too exhausted to say no. Plus, she thought it wise for the twins to have a strong, male figure back in their lives again.

A cool breeze ran through the line of freshly washed clothes and linens, rustling Annabelle out of her reminiscing. She saw Papa walk out the front door of the main house onto the porch. He put his fists on his hips, took a deep breath of fresh morning air, and smiled at the land in front of him. Papa started every day this way. He didn't know she was watching, but Annabelle enjoyed seeing her father complete this ritual each morning. It served the same purpose to her as a rooster's caw, a signal that the day has begun. He never saw, but she always took a breath with him and smiled back.

"Grandpa Joe! Grandpa Joe! Grandpa Joe!" one of the twins yelled as she spotted her grandfather emerging from the house. "Have you seen our dolls? Mama helped us make them. I named mine Daisy because that's my name and I think it's the prettiest name there is."

Her sister Eliza, not to be out done, sprinted from her place on the lawn to tell Grandpa Joe about her doll.

"Well my doll's name is Grandpa Joe. I named her after you, Grandpa, because I think you're the best grandpa there is."

"You can't name your doll after Grandpa! Your doll's a girl! You have to name her something pretty, like Clementine or Pearl."

"Nuh-uh. I can name her anything I want because she's my doll and I want to name her Grandpa Joe."

"Well my doll doesn't want to play with your doll anymore then!"

"Now, girls. No need for all this bickering. I think you picked out a couple of fine names for those little dolls of yours. Go on inside and wash yourselves up for breakfast. Wash your dolls up, too. I don't care what their names are as long as they've got manners."

The twins clutched their cornhusk dolls to their chests and scampered inside, fueled by their beloved grandfather's praise. Papa noticed Annabelle smiling to herself and pinning the last of the laundry to the line. He felt warmth spread over his whole body at the sight. It had been quite a while since he'd seen his daughter smile unprompted. She had always been an accommodating girl, so anytime a friend tried to cheer her up or make her laugh she'd always reward them with at least a smile, but he could tell she was almost always just going through the motions. This was a different kind of smile, however. She hadn't been asked or coerced. This smile was hers alone and it was a sight to see. He regretting having to interrupt whatever thought was causing it, but it was time for breakfast.

"Belle! Food's up! Come make sure your daughter's washed their hands like I asked them to."

"Alright, Papa. I'll be there in a moment, and you know perfectly well those four little hands are still covered in grime."

Papa chuckled and walked back inside. The house smelled like baking bread and salt. After Annabelle's mother died in childbirth, instead of finding a new wife or hiring help, Papa worked twice as hard to raise her and run his ranch. He had hired help to assist with the daily goings on of the ranch, but he insisted on taking care of Annabelle mostly on his own. His sisters would stay with him every once in a while, and some women in town would take pity on his situation and bring meals by, but Papa never took pity on himself. He would have done anything for his wife, and Annabelle deserved even more than that.

One skill he picked up along the way was cooking. He first started out of necessity, but soon came to think of it as a hobby. Even when Annabelle moved back onto the ranch he insisted on making every meal. Annabelle didn't mind. She preferred the chores that took her outside in the open air. Spending hours in a steamy kitchen always made her feel trapped.

This morning, Papa baked fresh cornbread, boiled eggs, and picked some fresh blackberries from the bush next to the house. It was lucky that there were any berries left to pick considering the twins' penchant for sneaking off in the afternoon to stuff themselves before dinner. Their sticky, juice covered mouths and purple fingers always gave them away. Papa walked into the kitchen and there they were, sticky and purple, guiltily averting their eyes away from the empty fruit bowl on the table.

"Daisy an Eliza, did you see who came in here and ate all the berries before breakfast?"

"No," Eliza responded quietly.

"It must have been Mama!" Daisy quickly offered.

"Oh, yes. It must have been, huh? Is your mama also the one who sneaks off to the blackberry bush before dinner then, too?"

The twins blushed with embarrassment in unison.

"Go wash your sticky little hands again before I make you eat the whole bush!" Grandpa Joe teased.

They giggled excitedly and jumped off their chairs to wash up for a second time before breakfast. They almost knocked the empty basket out of their mother's hands as they flew by.

"What was that all about?" Annabelle asked.

"The girls ate all the blackberries again. One of these days I oughtta punish them but I just don't know if I have it in me."

"They're good girls, Papa. I think they'll turn out okay even if you are a little soft on them."

"I was soft on you and you turned out all right."

"I guess I did. Although I do I have to sometimes fight the urge to sneak around back and steal a handful of berries."

Papa chuckled and started slicing the cornbread.

"It smells delicious, Papa. I don't know where you find the time to cook as well as everything else it is you do."

"Belle, you just gotta make time to do the things you love. It wouldn't hurt you to take a second for yourself every once in a while."

"I don't know if I could. There's so much to do around here and it wouldn't feel right to lounge around when you've been so kind as to let me and the girls come back here."

"Sweetheart, I'm glad for your help but you don't owe me a damn thing. You're my daughter and I'm supposed to take care of you, not the other way around. I want you to take the twins out to the pond later this afternoon. Sit in the sun and watch them swim for a while. You haven't stopped moving since you got here."

Annabelle didn't know if she could stop moving. It'd been two years since her husband's death, but every time she stood still for too long the memories would come flooding back fresh as ever. She couldn't tell her father this or else he'd worry, and she definitely didn't want to upset her girls. She'd do anything to make her father happy, though, so she decided to try it. If it became too much she'd just jump in the water with the twins. A quick splash in the icy pond would clear her mind right up.

"Okay, Papa. I'll take the twins swimming. It's turning out to be a beautiful day after all. Oh, but you should come, too! The girls would love that."

"Not today, I'm afraid. I'll be working on all the chores you'll be neglecting while you're out."

"You're such a tease! What a mean old man you've turned out to be," Annabelle returned with a joking smile.

"Eat up, dear. You'll need the extra energy to keep up with me."

***

After finishing up the last of her chores, Annabelle rounded up Daisy and Eliza. The girls fought about who got to wear their hair in braids and who in pigtails while their mother attempted to get them dressed in their bathing outfits. As Annabelle was slipping a shirt of Daisy's head she managed to grab hold of her sister's braid and give it a tug. Eliza began to cry.

"Girls, please. Do you want to go to the pond or do you want to stay here and clean the stables with Grandpa Joe? He could really use the help in there."

Eliza sniffled one last time and held back her tears.

"No!" she blurted, "I'm not crying. I want to go swimming."

"I'll be good," promised Daisy, "please take me to the pond."

"Alright, you can come with me. Grandpa Joe is going to be very disappointed."

On their way out the door, Papa stopped them to say a quick goodbye.

"Don't give your mother a hard time now. Who knows how long it will be until she finds another moment to relax."

"We won't," they replied in unison.

"Oh and Annabelle, please try not to give yourself a hard time either, okay?"

"I won't," she said with a sad smile.

Papa squeezed her shoulder once and headed off to the stables. The pond was only a short walk through the woods behind the family ranch. There was a fairly worn trail that Annabelle remembered walking along as a little girl. As she led her daughters down it she realized that she hadn't been on it since then. On warm summer days when they finished their chores early, Papa would take her to the pond. He wouldn't go in the water, he had never learned to swim, but he happily watched her splash around from the shore. She wondered if the old swinging rope they tied up together was still hanging.

The trio soon rounded the bend in the trail that signified that the pond was just up ahead. They walked into a small clearing that had an even smaller pool of still water right in the center. The swinging rope was still intact, hanging from the branch of a nearby oak. It was nearly silent, with the exception of the twins' excited feet and chirps of happiness. It was exactly how she remembered it with Papa.

"Mama! Look at the rope. Can we swing from it?"

"That rope's older than you are, Daisy. Let me give it a good tug before you accidently bring the whole forest down."

Eliza quietly and quickly slipped off her shoes and ran towards the pond. Annabelle could barely open her mouth to say, "Be careful!" before her daughter fearlessly jumped into the pool. Her little head of wet brown hair popped up out of the water and yelled, "It's freezing! Jump in, Daisy!" Daisy immediately forgot about the rope and sprinted towards her floating sister, shoes flying off as she ran. She disappeared into the water and surfaced seconds later behind Eliza.

"Boo!" she yelled, "I'm a pond monster and I'm going to eat you!"

Eliza screamed and swam away to the other side of the pond. Annabelle serenely watched her daughters chase each other in the water. She was pleasantly surprised at how normal it seemed. Maybe the twins were too young when their father died to really remember him now. Maybe she was the only one who still couldn't picture his face without tearing up. She felt small drop fall from her eye. This one wasn't a sad tear, though. For the first time in two years she felt like things might turn out all right.

Annabelle was able to relax comfortably in the grass for almost an hour before she was itching to get back to the ranch to work. She even closed her eyes for a minute and let the sun warm her cheeks. The girls had stopped chasing each other and were now floating on their backs and trying not to bump into each other. Annabelle figured it was probably close to dinnertime and they should go back.

"Daisy! Eliza! Jump on out, now. The sun's coming down and we gotta get back before Grandpa Joe eats supper without us."

The thought of missing out on a meal caused the twins to spring up out of the water and onto the shore. Annabelle had barely gotten to her feet before they had their shoes on and were running home through the woods. She lost sight of them just as they turned the bend, but she wasn't worried. One time was usually enough for those two to learn anything, and the trail was no exception. Annabelle took her time walking back. The forest was nostalgic and comforting, and she enjoyed listening to the wind blow through the leaves and the occasional chirp of a bird flying off. She was lost in thought when Daisy came running back down the trail toward her. She was crying so hard she almost tripped.

"Mama! You...you gotta hurry! Something happened to Grandpa Joe!"

Annabelle's peace was shattered immediately. She scooped up her sobbing daughter and bolted the rest of the way back to the ranch. When she got there, she saw Eliza crying on the porch being consoled by a woman from town. A crowd of people had gathered around the stables. Annabelle hugged Daisy and put her down with her sister before running into the crowd. Townspeople and farm hands were all there standing in front of the stable doors. She elbowed her way through the crowd and saw the local doctor kneeling over her father's unmoving body. His eyes were closed and it didn't look like he was breathing. Annabelle dropped to her knees.

"Papa!' she cried, shaking his leg with her hand in an attempt to wake him, " Papa, please wake up! You've gotta wake up!"

"Annabelle, I'm sorry, but you have to get back. I can't help your father if you don't let me," pleaded the doctor.

Annabelle wrung her hands as she watched the doctor check his pulse and throat but there wasn't much to be done. After what felt like hours, but was only a few minutes, the doctor leaned back and shook his head.

"I'm so sorry, Annabelle. I think he had a heart attack. There's nothing I can do."

Annabelle fell over her father's body and continued to sob. The people around her were silent at first, but soon began to dissipate. The doctor allowed her to grieve for a few more minutes before interjecting.

"Dear, we have to take the body. Your pa's gonna have the best damn funeral this side of the Mississippi, all right? I just have to get him ready for it."

"Please, not yet. I gotta let my girls say goodbye to their Grandpa Joe."

The doctor nodded and walked over to the porch to fetch the trembling twins. They only cried harder the closer they got to their grandfather's body.

"Girls," Annabelle squeaked out, "Grandpa Joe's had a heart attack. He's gonna be gone from his body soon but you can still say goodbye to him while a little piece is still here."

They were nervous to get too close at first, but this wasn't the first time they'd seen a dead body. Annabelle held out her hands to her daughters and pulled them in close. The three of them cried over the wonderful man who went out of his way to give them a better life. The twins hugged their grandfather one last time before running back into the skirts of the woman on the porch. Annabelle held her father's hand and took a deep breath.

"Papa, I know when you get up there the first thing you're gonna want to do is find Mama. Give her big hug for me when you do, okay? And then after that will you go see Arnold and tell him that I miss him and his daughter's are growing up beautifully? He's gonna be worried about us now that you're gone, but I want you both to know I'm gonna be strong this time. For me and for them," she gave his hand a squeeze. "I love you, Papa. Sleep sweet."

The doctor patted her on the shoulder as she stood up, face in her hands.

"Why don't you go on inside with your girls. Me and the boys will take care of your father. When they saw him lying on the ground like that they jumped on their horses and came right out to get me. They couldn't have gone any faster. You've got yourself some good boys working for you, that's for sure."

"Thanks, doctor. Be good to him."

"Of course I will, Annabelle."

Annabelle walked towards the house and couldn't bring herself to look back. She had to stay strong for Daisy and Eliza and if she turned around now she didn't think she'd be able to do it. When she got to the porch she thanked the townswoman for taking care of her daughters and told her she should head home, despite the woman's offer to stay and help with dinner. Annabelle ushered her daughters inside, made them a lackluster dinner, and sent them off to bed. She lay down in her own bed soon after, but wouldn't fall asleep until almost dawn.

***

Annabelle was awoken by a knock at the door. She almost stayed in bed thinking that her father would answer but then remembered what had happened the day before. Her feet felt like lead as she swung them onto the floor and her robe was just as heavy. When she opened the front door a small man in a dusty, but well made, suit was waiting for her. He had bushy gray mustache and hair to match that peeked out from underneath his hat. He was holding a leather briefcase in one hand, and the other was extended out to meet her.

"How do you do, Miss Annabelle?" The man moved his hand a little closer to her until she realized that he was looking for a handshake. "My name's Mr. Turner, Darren Turner, and I'm your father's attorney and executor of his will. Do you have a moment to sit down with me? There's a lot to discuss."

Annabelle was a bit taken aback but invited Mr. Turner into the kitchen. He sat down at the kitchen table and began taking papers out of his briefcase. Annabelle sat down across from him and waited in silence. Mr. Turner spent about five minutes shuffling and arranging his papers before he spoke up abruptly.

"Miss Annabelle, your father has left equal shares of his estate to you and your two daughters, Daisy and Eliza, but he has also left equal shares to a man named Derek Hardin and his two children, Charles and Silas Hardin–"

"What?" she interrupted, "Who on God's green Earth is Derek Hardin and why is my father leaving him money?"

"Now, hold on there, Miss Annabelle. I'm not quite finished. Everyone gets their fair share of the estate if you all can live together on this ranch for six whole months. You'll continue to run the ranch as usual and Derek will take over working in the stables and taking care of the horses. You'll have to share this house with him and his boys."

"There's no way in hell I'm doing that."

"Miss Annabelle, please. Language. You're gonna have to do it or else you and your daughters won't see a dime."

"Where did my father meet this Derek Hardin? How come I've never heard of him before?"

"All I know is he lives a couple towns over. It's only him and his sons, apparently a widower. I'm headed there next to tell him about this arrangement. Now I suggest you spend today getting this place ready for three more people, as I don't suspect he will pass up the offer. Your father was not a poor man. I'll be back to check up on you sporadically to make sure you're still upholding the requirements of Joe's will. Good day, Miss Annabelle."

Annabelle was still reeling long after her father's lawyer had left. How could her father give half of what he owned to a stranger and his family? Even more so, how could he ask her to share her home with him? And if she refused, she and her daughters were out on the street. She began questioning everything she thought she knew about the man who she thought would do anything for her. She was only pulled out of this train of thought once Daisy and Eliza got out of bed. They shuffled into the kitchen, knelt by their mother and put their heads in her lap. Annabelle softly cooed as she stroked their hair.

"Shh, girls. Everything's going to be all right."

"But who's going to make breakfast?" Eliza whimpered.

"I will, of course, and you two are going to help me. Would you like that?"

The twins perked up and nodded. Grandpa Joe loved the twins, but when he cooked breakfast he liked to be alone. It was the only time of the day he required a little peace and quiet. Annabelle lit the stove and handed Eliza a bowl of eggs to scramble. Daisy busied herself by slicing the rest of the cornbread left over from yesterday's breakfast. She split the slices evenly amongst three plates, but left one slice on the tray "for Grandpa Joe." Once everything was finished cooking, the trio sat down for a mostly quiet meal. The meeting with her father's lawyer weighed heavily on Annabelle's shoulders, however, and it wasn't long before she told the twins what tomorrow had in store.

"Girls, I've got something to tell you. We might not be the only ones on this ranch for very long."

"What do you mean?" questioned Daisy.

"Well, before Grandpa Joe passed he wrote a letter saying what to do with all of his things when he went, and in that letter he said that half of his things belonged to a man named Derek Hardin and his sons, but only if we all live on the ranch together for a while. Mr. Hardin is going to look after Grandpa Joe's horses and his sons, Charles and Silas, will help you girls out with the chores. That also means you're gonna have to go back to sharing a room just like at our old farm."

"That's not fair! I don't want to share with Eliza. She snores!"

"Why do we have to share our house with them anyways?"

"Because if we don't then we don't get to stay on the ranch anymore. Do you want that? Do you want to go out and start begging on the streets? Do you?"

"No, Mama," Daisy replied sheepishly.

Annabelle felt guilty for lashing out at her daughters, but the stress of it all overcame her. She took a couple more bites of her breakfast before she calmed down.

"I'm sorry I yelled at you."

"It's okay, Mama. I know you're just sad like when Papa died."

Annabelle was caught off guard. Eliza hadn't mentioned her father once since he passed. Daisy talked about him at first, but slowly stopped after a while. It was foolish of her to think that they didn't remember him.

"Yes, baby. It's just like that. And it's okay for you to be sad, too."

"I am, but not like then. I know Grandpa Joe didn't mean to leave us, not like Papa."

"Eliza, Papa didn't leave us on purpose. Why do you think that?"

"Because Papa said 'goodbye' before he left. He knew he wasn't coming back."

"Papa said 'goodbye' like he always did. He didn't know he wouldn't see you again."

"It wasn't the same kind of 'goodbye,' Mama. I could tell."

Annabelle didn't realize how much about her father's death Eliza had realized. She was only six-years-old at the time and Annabelle thought she couldn't possibly have grasped the fact that her father killed himself. She barely understood the concept herself. Daisy didn't chime in, but she could see in her eyes that she understood, too. Annabelle stayed silent instead of trying to convince her daughters otherwise, but that only confirmed what they already knew. *These girls are too smart for their own good*, Annabelle thought.

Annabelle and her daughter's went about their day almost normally. They completed their chores, checked in on the horses–Annabelle had given the stable boys the day off to grieve even if she refused to take one–and moved all of Eliza's things into Daisy's room, despite Daisy's vocal protests. When Annabelle tucked the girls in for the night she told them not to worry, but she didn't know if she was saying it more for them or for herself.

***

The next morning, Annabelle made sure to be up bright and early as to not be surprised by any expected or unexpected guests. It didn't take long before there was another knock at the door. When she answered it she was greeted by a man who was almost the complete opposite of the man graced her doorstep the day before. Derek Hardin was tall, rugged, and his clothes were no suit, but fit him nicely just the same. He wore a dark Stetson on top of a head of even darker hair. Two small boys that looked like softer versions of their father peeked out from behind his legs.

"Are you Miss Annabelle Colt?"

"Yes, sir, the very same. And you must be Mr. Derek Hardin and company."

"That would be me, ma'am. It seems me and my boys are supposed to come and stay with you for a while."

"It seems so."

Annabelle stood her ground and looked Derek straight in the eye. She knew this was coming, but still couldn't help but feel protective over what she saw as her ranch.

"Mind if we come in? My boys are excited to meet you and the twins."

The boys smiled up at her. Charles was a bit taller and presumably older, but Silas still had a youthful glint in his eye and a bright smile that Annabelle couldn't help but be softened by.

"All right, you can come in."

She almost said "Make yourselves at home," but she wasn't ready to be that friendly quite yet.

"Daisy! Eliza! Come meet Mr. Hardin and his boys."

The twins scurried into the living room, much more excited about their new housemates than their mother. The twins rarely ever saw boys their age, let alone lived with them, and they were positively giddy. The sisters held hands and whispered in each other's ears as they giggled.

"Well, introduce yourselves."

"Hello, Mr. Hardin, Charles, Silas, I'm Eliza Colt. It's very nice to meet you."

"And I'm Daisy!" she gave a clumsy curtsey before falling back into a fit of giggles with Eliza.

The Hardin boys shyly introduced themselves with just their names and never got closer to the twins than they needed to be.

"Hi, Miss Daisy and Miss Eliza, my name's Mr. Derek and I'm very happy that you're allowing me and my sons to stay with you in your home."

The twins were already enamored with all three of the Hardin boys and couldn't muster up any response but an excited smile. Annabelle softly rolled her eyes at her precocious daughters and shooed them into the kitchen.

"Let me show you your rooms."

The young boys took to their new room immediately. They happily decided who would sleep in which bed and bounced on top of them excitedly. Annabelle took Derek to her father's old room. At first, she was concerned about letting a stranger sleep in his bed, but quickly decided that it would just be too painful to do it herself.

"And this will be your room, Mr. Hardin. I hope you find it to your liking."

"It's cozy, Miss Colt. Thank you for your hospitality."

Annabelle left him with a nod and went to the kitchen to start preparing breakfast. The twins had already begun cracking eggs and making dough, encouraged by yesterday's meal prep. Annabelle felt happy that her daughters were reacting so well to having the Hardin boys come to stay. She might not have been wholeheartedly welcoming, but that didn't mean she wasn't going to be a good host. While the girls prepared the food, Annabelle set the table for six. She called the boys to the table once they finished cooking. The children sat on either side of the table, coyly smiling at each other and then immediately looking away. Annabelle sat at the head of the table, where her father used to sit, and Derek sat at the other end.

"So, Mr. Hardin, how did you know my father?"

"I saved his life."

"I've never heard about this. What are you talking about?"

"It was almost five years ago now. I was in town picking up some supplies when I saw your father standing near by. A man had lost control of his horse and it was headed straight for him. I ran over and pushed your father out of the way before that horse could trample him to death. After that he bought me a drink at the saloon and we got to talking. We kept in touch until his passing. I figured the drink was enough to thank me, but it seems like he wanted to give me more."

"Papa never told me about that and he never once mentioned you. How do I know you're not lying?"

"Why would I lie? I had to have met the man somehow or else I wouldn't be here."

Annabelle stayed quiet when she realized he was right. The rest of breakfast was mostly silent except for the occasional whisper and laugh between the two girls. After the meal, Annabelle took Derek out to the stable to meet the horses while the children cleaned up the kitchen. The family owned four horses that they mostly used to get to and from town.

"This here's Scout. He was Papa's favorite horse. He's almost too old to ride now, but Papa insisted on taking care of his horses until their final day, useful or not."

"It's very nice to meet you, Scout."

Derek reached out his hand and touched the old horse on the nose. Scout pressed his face against his palm and whinnied softly. Annabelle was surprised at how gently this rough looking man approached the horse. He soothingly hushed the animal as he walked around it, one hand stroking his back. She wondered how that hand would feel on her face and felt herself blush at the thought. She couldn't believe that she was having feelings about this stranger she's being forced to live with.

"I have to go start the day's chores. Please do the same in here."

Annabelle turned on her heel and hurried back into the house. She didn't want Derek to see her flustered. He stayed out in the stables for most of the day while she fluttered around the ranch trying to keep herself busy so she wouldn't think about him. This went on for a couple weeks. All six of them would sit down for meals together, but during the day Annabelle did her best to avoid Derek. After a month of this, Derek pulled her aside.

"Annabelle, I know you didn't ask for us to be here but I'm wondering if I've wronged you anyway else? You don't seem to want to give me the time of day."

"Oh, no, that's not it. I'm sorry, Derek. I'm just...very busy. Running a ranch is a lot of work even with your help."

"Okay," Derek replied, unconvinced, "if you're sure that's all."

"That's all."

Annabelle still wasn't ready to tell him that he already spent so much time in her thoughts that seeing him in person during the day seemed excessive. She hadn't felt this way about a man since her husband died. In some ways, Annabelle had resigned herself to a life alone with her daughters. She thought she was happy with that, but having a man around the house again was comforting. She had to keep reminding herself that at the end of these six months he'd no longer be living there. The thought bothered her more than she expected it to. Derek had already started to walk away when Annabelle stopped him.

"Actually, Derek, there is something else."

"What is it?"

"Sometimes you chew too loudly during supper. It gets on my last nerve."

Derek chuckled and said, "I'll work on that."

Annabelle couldn't bring herself to tell Derek about her feelings for him. She had no idea if he even felt the same way and didn't want to make the rest of their time on the ranch uncomfortable. She decided that it would be best to keep her feelings to herself, even if they were growing stronger each day.

***

The remaining months began to fly by. The two families living side by side eventually felt normal for Annabelle. She almost didn't realize that the sixth month was about to come to an end when Mr. Turner showed up on their doorstep.

"Miss Annabelle, lovely to see you again. I hope things are well here?"

"Very much so, Mr. Turner. Please, come in."

"Oh no need for that this time. I've just come to remind you that this is the final week of your father's six-month request. Soon I'll be able to officially grant you your share of your father's estate. Would you mind Mr. Hardin of this as well? He'll be back to his own homestead soon I imagine."

"Yes, of course. It's been surprisingly nice to have him and the boys here these last few months. I'll be sorry to see them go."

"I imagine it's been comforting to have a man around after your father's passing."

"It has."

"Well, I'm off. Nice talking to you as always, Miss Annabelle. Oh! I almost forgot. Your father wanted me to give you this letter at the end of the six months."

Annabelle took the letter from Mr. Turner and shut the door. She unfolded it and read. Her eyes filled with tears as she got to the end. She dropped the letter on the floor and immediately went looking for Derek. He wasn't in the house or in the stables. The children were chasing each other around the yard but Derek was nowhere to be seen.

"Boys, have you seen your father?"

"He went walking in the woods behind the house!"

Annabelle sprinted down the path toward the pond. She was out of breath but couldn't stop running. When she got to the pond she found Derek sitting on the shore tossing stones into the water.

"Derek! What are you doing out here," she asked, winded.

"I'm going to be honest, Annabelle. The thought of leaving this ranch and you and the girls behind is awfully upsetting. I came out here to clear my head and think of a way to tell you that I'd like to stay, but you found me before I could think of anything better than that."

Annabelle couldn't wait another second. She closed the distance between the two of them, threw her arms around his neck, and kissed him.

"Derek, you're not going anywhere. Papa knew this was going to happen."

"What do you mean?"

"He wrote me a letter that said when he met you he knew you were the man for me, but I was married at the time. He secretly kept in touch with you in case something happened to my husband and when he passed, put this will together to make sure we met in case he died before getting to introduce us. He was so confident that we'd end up together that he left half of his estate to you and your boys."

"Your father was a great man, Annabelle. I just didn't know how great until now."

Derek lifted her up by the waist and kissed her passionately once more. The two of them would go on to get married and raise their four kids on the family ranch. Papa was gone, but by no means forgotten. Even in death, Papa made sure to take care of his girl.

FOR A FIREFIGHTER'S HEART

MARISA MEYER

Chapter 1

Christine Rossouw assessed the destruction left behind by the blaze that reduced the Mulders' house to nothing but a pile of rubble and ash. It was pure luck that no one had gotten hurt in the blaze. The fire had started in the early hours of the morning when the Mulders' were still fast asleep. Now they all stood on the sidewalk, with nothing but the clothes on their back and their pet cat Malfoy, looking in horror at what was left of their home. Their belongings and their memories had literally gone up in flames. Now that was something she could never fathom, why would a family who lived day to day, turning over every penny have to endure such hardships? Why could this not happen to someone who could afford it?

It's the Lord's way to test our faith; her father's voice reminded her. To her it was more an excuse used by churchgoers to explain away logic, and logic told her a long time ago, that man's path is not destined or designed by God, but that man's path is a series of truth or dares onramps to new beginnings and disastrous endings.

She ducked under the warning tape that stretched across the front lawn, here and there, there were a few firefighters ambling around, just to ensure that the fire had been completely snuffed. Her job was to investigate the cause of the fire and fill our mounds of paperwork for insurance claims. She stepped over what used to be the threshold of the house, into what was left of it. Everything was charred black, logically, if the Mulders had all been asleep, and still managed to get down the stairs and out the front door, the fire could only have started at the back of the house or possibly the basement. Instinctively she traipsed over the rubble making her way through to the back of the house where the Laundry area used to be.

It took her close to an hour to determine the area where the blaze started and another hour to determine if it was accidental or not.

In no time she had drawn the conclusion that the fire started as an electrical short in the laundry area. Apparently, Mrs. Mulder often left her tumble dryer on overnight. This, of course, would make claiming insurance a little more troublesome. Yet another flaw in the system, the insurance company is going to find every reason not to pay out the claim, by basing it on negligence, no wonder people were so up in arms with short term insurance places.

When she finally walked into her office by noon, she was finished, it's been one of those days where you barely get time to drink a cup of coffee, much less have lunch. The thought of lunch made her tummy rumble and she turned left down the hall to where the company's cafeteria was. She never ate here, but today was an exception. She had been up since 4 AM after being called out by the Fire Chief, and right now a greasy Burrito even sounded like heaven.

When she got back to her desk, there was a note that read – *Love me tender love me true, why not date me until you're blue.*

"Okay, guys! Who did it?" she asked as she crumpled up the note and dumped it in the trash.

None of them owned up but all of them laughed behind their sleeves. She knew that they all thought she was the odd one out, not being interested in dating and all. Whenever there was a company function that allowed partners, she went alone. If they all went out to drinks, she went alone. Now, it wasn't because she was anti the whole prospect of dating; it was just that she had no interest in getting tied down to one person who eventually ends up changing your character.

She had seen it so often. People lose their individuality, they change, and not for the better either, and years down the line, one or the other regret the fact that they had changed, and that's when trouble spoils paradise. Obviously, her current outlook on life came at a price. Just out of college, she dated Darryl, who was a very responsible young man with high ideals and in her opinion far-fetched dreams, but he was nice. In the beginning, like every other relationship, they both had different interests, but they both tried to get involved, she went with him to Nascar races, and he went with her to theater performances. Then they started to get comfortable and suddenly she was going to all the car races, and he came up with every excuse under the sun not to go to a theater. But it got worse, slowly but surely he started to get his back up whenever she went to the theater alone and then they ended up fighting more than anything. It was there when she finally pulled the plug on their relationship and promised herself never to date again, against her mother and fathers' wishes of course.

The ringing of her phone, drew her out of her train of thought and she reached for the receiver, "Rossouw speaking," she answered absentmindedly while she shuffled through the stack of paperwork on her desk.

"Oh, hey dad," she said and pinched the received between her shoulder and her ear. "Mmm no, I haven't forgotten... yeah... mmm... well, I'm kind of busy... I know, I said I would be there but something came up... seriously, dad, it's not like the church is going to run away... Okay fine, I'll be there... yeah, I love you too."

She pulled out the incident report from one of the arson cases she had to submit to the lawyer and shoved it into the out basket, then dropped her head on her arms. She loved her parents, but her dad was forever begging her to go to church. Another place she tries to avoid at all cost. Church people were probably the most hypocritical beings alive, she thought despondently, but she knew that if she went to this one service, they would leave her alone for several months before they begged her to visit again. So she was going to simply suck it up, go, and get it over and done with.

Chapter 2

Jarod looked at himself in the mirror as he fixed his tie, it was still a while before the church would start, but he preferred to be the first one in and the first one out, usually picking the last pew right in the corner. He had a very trying time after his divorce, nearly lost his job and everything he had, because of it. Was it not for Pastor Rossouw who helped him to see the light, he would still be staring at the bottom of the bottle. He was never much of a drinker during his marriage, but after he found out that Elaine cheated on him, he drowned his sorrows, the only way he knew how. It's been two years since they went their separate ways and it was just like Pastor Rossouw had said, his hatred had turned to indifference, and the love he once felt for Elaine had subsided. He often saw her in town, but there was no more anger or bitterness. The point is that they were two different people, and in the end, they simply drifted apart. Elaine wanted kids and a house with a white picket fence, two dogs, and an SUV, with a husband that worked nine to five. He couldn't give her that, not at the time anyway. So, as a result, she went out and found what she wanted. He was happy for her, he truly was, but he promised himself that he would never marry again and committed himself to the fact that he would focus on work and God.

"Morning Jarod," Pastor Rossouw greeted as he unlocked the church.

"Morning Pastor, lovely day today, isn't it?"

"Indeed, we need the rain; hopefully it's here to stay for a few days."

The unexpected gift of rain had been a blessing after weeks of drought and unbearable heat, and although the rainy season was still a few weeks ago, the skies didn't lie. Jarod loved the rain.

"According to the weather, we can expect rainfall for at least three days," he chuckled and then entered the church and waited for the pastor to turn the lights on.

"Are you going to move up a pew?" Pastor Rossouw asked.

Jarod shook his head and smiled, "Maybe next time."

The pastor didn't push him, but he always asked him out of interest more than anything, that was the extent of their conversations. More small talk really. The pastor went on about his business and Jarod took a seat in his usual spot, waiting patiently for the pews to fill up.

Today, however, with the rain falling, he didn't expect the church to be packed. He always found it rather odd how people would run about in the rain to get to Walmart or go places, but the moment it rains they use it as an excuse to skip church.

One by one individual and families arrived, filling the pews from the front of the church towards the back. Two youngsters came bolting down the side aisle and darted between a couple talking in the front, then they disappeared under the pews. No one seemed to be perturbed by their playfulness, which he liked. Then again the sign right above the small stage read – Let the little children come to me, and do not hinder them.

He turned his attention back to the small hymnal in his hands, and paged aimlessly through it, trying to appear preoccupied, in the hope that no-one tried to make any conversation with him. But his hopes were dashed with Pastor Rossouw spoke next to him.

"Jarod, I would like you to meet Christine, my daughter."

Jarod stood up and wiped his hand on the back of his jeans and then extended it to the woman in front of him. She was beautiful, tall with long blond hair that flowed loosely over her shoulders. But the smile that tugged at the corner of her lips didn't reach her light blue eyes. It was as if the lights were on but nobody was home, she was just going through the motions.

"It's a pleasure to meet you, Christine," he said and shook her hand firmly.

"It's a pleasure," she repeated his words and removed her hand.

"Jarod is a firefighter, I thought you two would have a lot in common," Pastor Rossouw piped up and Jarod wanted to shrink away, but he remained poised.

"You're also in the department?" he asked out of interest.

"Not exactly, I'm in forensics, I investigate the aftermath and the cause of the fire," she answered.

"Nice," he said, not sure what else to add.

He felt awkward with her, not in a negative kind of way, but purely because he hasn't spoken to a woman on a casual basis since before he was married. And when the pastor walked away leaving the two of them alone in each other's company, he shrugged and stepped back.

"You can sit here if you want?" he offered.

This time she smiled, "I won't mind at all, anything but sitting right in the front where my dad wants me."

Jarod chuckled and moved over two spaces, leaving enough space between them. They sat in silence for a while before Christine spoke.

"You have to excuse my dad, he can be very forward at times," she smiled, "He keeps wanting to set me up for dates."

Jarod laughed at that, "Playing pastor and matchmaker, I see."

She rolled her eyes, "Yeah, he does it every time I set foot in a church, which is why I'm never here," she turned to look at him, "I haven't seen you here before, though."

He shrugged, "I've been here a few months now, but I don't stay around to mingle with the members. I just come for my daily bread and then I disappear."

"Ah, I see," she said, "The dash and go type."

"Yeah, that would be me."

"You do know that church is meant for communion and encouragement from fellow Christians."

He leaned forward with his elbows on his knees and regarded the congregation, "I come here to learn and find peace."

"A man with depth, well I'm sure you'll find peace being stuck here in the back all the time."

"It's worked so far."

Throughout the service, Jarod was acutely aware of the woman who was seated next to him. The aroma of her perfume kept wafting past him, making him shift uncomfortably in his seat. By the time the service came to an end, he couldn't wait to get out. He needed fresh air and fast.

"Well Jarod, it was a nice having company here at the back," Christine said as she stood up to let him pass.

"Yeah, it was," he dragged his hand over his stubbly short hair, "I'll see you around?"

All she did was nod, and that was his queue. He exited this church like a bolt of lightning.

Chapter 3

Christine did not expect that at all. She knew her father was up to something when he insisted on her coming to church. She was prepared for the worst, him introducing her to another pastor, or one of the deacons, or worst case, preaching hellfire and brimstone to try and get her to get back into the habit of going to church. The last thing she expected was to be introduced to a firefighter. And not just any firefighter, Jarod Marks had all the bits and pieces that would make any woman turn into a fan-girl. He was built like an MMA fighter, he had deep willow green eyes and brown, almost black hair that was neatly trimmed and on top of that, he had that five o'clock shadow that danced across his chin, making him look even manlier than he possibly could. For the first time in years, she wondered if her anti-dating motto was even viable. Just because she made one bad choice in life, by dating Darryl, didn't mean that every man she met would be like him.

After the service, she had spoken to her dad and tried to find out more about Jarod, of course, her dad was all too happy to tell her that he's a firefighter, with a deep soul, but beyond that, he didn't want to divulge any personal information. He did, however, mention that Jarod had also been in a bad relationship that left him weary of dating, much like her.

So what if he was damaged goods, she, though, he couldn't possibly be more damaged than she was.

Thankfully thinking about Jarod and the possibility of entering the dating scene again was a momentarily lapse in judgment, but the next day, she had once again gotten her mind focused on work and making sure she didn't fall into the dating trap again. Or so she thought. Every now and again, when she wasn't going through case files or looking at labs of fire starters that contained possible chemicals, Jarod's face floated into her mind. It got to a point where she went for her second visit to the cafeteria in one week, which was totally out of character. This time she opted for a slice of cheesecake and strong coffee.

"Rossouw!" one of her colleagues called. "Having a love affair with that cheesecake?"

"Shut it, Kemp," she mumbled and took a generous scoop out of spite and shoved it all into her mouth.

Dalton Kemp came over and pulled the chair out, plonking himself down, "You really need to get out more, we're having a get-together tonight at Franks' are you coming around?"

Franks was a bar not too far from the office, where they staff often went to wind down after a rough day at the office. Most of the time she opted out of going to mingle, but tonight was an exception, she needed a distraction.

"Yeah sure, I'll see you there at around seven."

"Great, bring your date," Kemp chuckled and dug her coffee spoon into her cheesecake.

"Hey! Stop that," she muttered and pulled her plate away.

One thing about her line of work and the people she worked with was that they were all like family. And this was the only family where she felt she belonged. Back at home, with her mom and dad, she felt like the odd one out, simply because she didn't share in their beliefs. She used to, but it all changed in her first year of being a firefighter. It was during that year, where she realized that God helps who he wants to. She had seen too many tragic deaths that included young children and elderly people to think that there was anything merciful about God. After a year of being a firefighter, she eventually opted to take a job in forensics and fire investigations and was transferred. Now instead of running into burning buildings to save people, she now investigated the aftermath instead.

At around noon, after her last case file was concluded, she locked her office and made her way to Franks' to join the others. The atmosphere was festive and the place was crowded. She spotted her colleagues at the far end near the back of the pup and wrangled her way through the crowd.

"Rossouw! You made it, where's Mr. Cheesecake?" Kemp called out raising his beer to her.

She rolled her eyes and laughed, "We had a fight, I left him in the cafeteria to bond with Miss Caramel," she joked.

She ordered herself a cola since she wasn't really one for drinking and joined the rest. The mood was light, and no one spoke about work, which was a relief. She opted for a seat at the far end of the table next to Janet, the receptionist, who was a gray little mouse who barely spoke as it was. She was a bit of an introvert, so other than sipping on her drink she didn't add much value to the conversation. But Christine didn't mind that at all.

It was a while later when a sudden explosion ripped through the kitchen and an orange flame punched its way into the main bar area. Windows shattered and people fell to the ground as smoke and fire billowed into the establishment. Caroline grabbed Jannet and pulled her down to the ground almost instantly as panic erupted. Everywhere people were trying to make it out of the bar, some managing just before the flames engulfed the front entrance.

"Bathroom!" Christine cried out as she tugged Janet's arm, practically dragging her along the side of the wall towards the back where the restrooms were. With any luck they could find a way out through one of the small windows, worst cases they would have water.

The fire alarms erupted over and above the agonizing cries of everyone stuck in the building and Christine knew that if they made it out of here alive, it would be a miracle. Her hope to find an escape route through one of the smaller windows was futile, she might fit through one at a squeeze but Janet won't and she refused to leave the young girl behind. Huddled in the corner of the bathroom, with her arms wrapped around the frantic girl, she could only hope that someone will get to them in time. For the first time in years, she prayed for help.

Christine thought fast, she pulled off her top and drenched it with water, then handed it to Janet, "Here, keep this over your mouth and nose, try to take shallow breaths okay?"

She then grabbed her denim jacket and did the same. Smoke was starting to fill the bathroom and the heat from the main room was slowly pushing towards the back. Time was of the essence, and if the fire department did not arrive soon, they would all meet their maker.

"We're going to die!" Janet panicked.

"No we're not, help is on its way," Christine shouted over the noise of crackling flames and falling banisters.

The sound of approaching sirens was a relief to some extent, at least the fire department was here, but the question that plagued her, was if they would get to them in time. Christine assessed their situation.

The fire hadn't reached the restrooms yet, but the heat was excruciating, and smoke pummeled into the small room stealing all the oxygen. She instructed Janet to stay put while she crawled out from under the sink, keeping her body bowed low on the ground. She needed to get to one of the windows and call for help. She felt her way around the floor until she reached one of the cubicles, and then she clambered her way to the window.

"Help! We're in here!" she shouted between bouts of coughs and heaving for air. Her throat was burning and her lungs were filled with smoke, but she refused to give up, "Help!" she called again and again.

"Over here!" she heard someone shout and only then did she allow herself to collapse on the floor. At least now someone would try to get to them.

The last thing she remembered was the incessant smoke that filled the room and the unbearable heat that licked at her skin before her entire world went black.

"Christine! Stay with me!" she recognized the voice from somewhere but she couldn't quite place it, "Christine can you hear me?"

She tried to respond but she simply couldn't. Her brain was doing all the work but the signal to the rest of her body was down. She kept drifting in and out of consciousness but the cool air that surrounded her meant that she was no longer in the inferno. That, or she had died and gone to, wherever bad girls go.

"Where is the ambulance!" she heard her savior call out.

"J... Janet," she managed to utter.

"She's responsive! Christine, it's Jarod, you've had some smoke inhalation, do you know where you are?" she heard him asked.

She tried to open her eyes, but it felt like a million cinders were stuck to her eyeballs, "Where is Janet," she asked first and foremost.

"She's fine, she's alive, thanks to you," he said and squeezed her hand, "But now we need to take care of you."

"Jarod?" she asked half deliriously, "From church?"

He chuckled and brushed her hair from her face, "Yeah Jarod from church, now save your breath. The ambulance will take you to the hospital; I'll come by later to check up on you."

She reached blindly for his hand and squeezed it, "Thank you," she whispered as her head spun and she once again plummeted into a dark hole.

Chapter 4

Jarod was the first to arrive at the hospital, followed by Christine's mom and dad, who both looked like they had been crying.

"Pastor Rossouw..." Jarod started.

"Call me James," he said to Jarod and then introduced his wife, "This is Marjorie, have you heard anything?"

He shook his head, "No I haven't, I'm not family but I know that she had inhaled a lot of smoke, but thankfully the fire never reached them."

"Oh thank you, Lord," her mother exclaimed casting her eyes to the heavens.

"Christine was very brave," Jarod said as he told the couple how she burrowed into the restrooms with her colleague, using very basic methods to keep from suffocating, "When she decided to call for help, was when she inhaled most of the smoke. But if she hadn't done that, no one would have known they were in the bathroom."

Marjorie sat down and cupped her hand over her mouth and James sat down beside her, wrapping his arm around her shoulders, "You were heaven sent," he said to Jarod, "Thank you for saving our little girl."

Jarod smiled and shook his head, "I was just doing my duty sir Pastor."

He left the couple and made his way down the corridor to get some coffee, he was still in uniform, covered in soot and smelling like a furnace, but he didn't want to go until he was a hundred percent sure that Christine was out of danger.

A while later he returned and made his way to where Christine's room was, through the window he saw the Pastor and his wife talking to Christine, who looked like hell but beautiful all the same. She was alive, and by the looks of it, recovering. Thankfully she didn't sustain any burns, it could have been so much worse.

Christine had spotted him just as he was about to leave and waved him over. When he entered the room, her mom and dad excused themselves to go get a bite to eat.

"How are you feeling?" he asked as he pulled a chair closer.

"Like a pizza base right out of the oven?" she said and laughed, but then coughed and clutched her chest, "change that, I feel like I've been to hell and back."

Jarod chuckled and handed her a glass of water, "It was quite something you did back there, your dad mentioned to me you were a firefighter before."

She took a sip of water and counted her breaths, "Yeah, for a year, then I moved to fire forensics."

"I'm glad you didn't forget the training then, it came in handy," he commented.

Even as she lay there, pale as a sheet, with her blond hair still covered in soot and ash, she was beautiful. He never thought that he would even look at another woman after his wife cheated on him, and here he was, doing just that.

He cleared his throat and made an effort to leave, but Christine caught his arm, and smiled, "I owe you dinner and a movie," she said half smiling.

He chuckled and nodded, "As soon as you're back on your feet, I'll come to collect."

Soon he was ushered away when the nurses entered to do the general BP checks, but for a moment he stood looking at her over their heads.

"And the Lord God said, It is not good that a man should be alone," a disembodied voice sounded and Jarod turned to respond, but there was no one else around, other than the nurses going about their business.

Puzzled he turned and looked back at Christine and then waved and left. This was the strangest thing he had ever experienced. It was as if there was someone else there with him, someone far more enlightened than he was. But the words stuck to him all the way home. And he realized beyond a shadow of a doubt that Christine did not appear in his life out of mere coincidence. This was something far bigger than him, or anyone else for that matter.

Chapter 5

Within a few days, Christine was discharged from hospital and sent home to recover. On her mother's insistence, she had no choice but to spend another week staying her folks until she was strong enough to return to work, but every day, Jarod made an effort to visit her, and if he couldn't get to her physically, he would call her. At first, she thought nothing of it, assuming that he was simply being nice, but out of the blue, every time her phone rang and his caller ID flickered on her screen, her stomach would rumble with excitement. Or when she heard his car pull up, she could hardly contain herself. Her dad, of course, wasn't blind either. He knew exactly what was going on.

"Jarod's a fine young man," he said one morning over coffee.

"Yeah, he's nice," she mumbled into her cup.

"Do you like him?"

She whipped her head around and looked at her dad, but the way he smiled at her disarmed her completely and she felt a blush creep into her cheeks, "Yeah, a little."

Her dad chuckled, and Christine put her cup down, "How do you know when you meet the right person?" she asked.

Her dad took his reading glasses off and regarded her, "That's a tough one on answer sweetheart, but sometimes you just know."

She worried her lip and looked into the distance. She had spent all this time guarding her own heart against heartbreak and disappointment. For so long she refused to believe that love existed and convinced herself that she didn't need anyone to go home too. But tragedy has a way to open one's eyes and this is exactly what happened to her. While she was trapped in that restroom practically staring death in the face, her first instinct was to pray and ask God to help her and Janet out of that pickle. It was at that point where she remembered to use what she had to her advantage. And not once during that entire time while they were stuck in that room did she panic, it was an ethereal calm that had taken over and now that she has had time to think it over, she could only come to one conclusion. God had sent His angels to help them. And she was convinced that Jarod was one of them, her personal angel. The thought of him warmed up her heart and a smile spread across her face.

"Penny for your thoughts?" her dad asked.

"I think it's time I go back to church," she said, "and I think I want to give love a chance."

Her dad put his book down and turned to her, smiling, "It's only when you leap into the water that you learn to swim sweetheart. Trust in the Lord and he will make a way clear for you."

Her dad always had wise comebacks, and although she still had a lot to overcome, she knew that little baby steps would eventually get her there.

At around noon, Jared's car rumbled outside, and Christine gave herself one last once-over in the mirror. It was date night, and she was nervous. She tucked a stray strand of hair back into place pulled her lips into a tight pout and released it. It felt as if the muscles in her face were refusing to cooperate.

"Honey!" her mom called and she took a deep steadying breath before making her way to the living room.

When she saw Jared, her heart did that familiar tumble, "Hi," she said and mentally rolled her eyes at her own silliness, "I mean, welcome?" she shook her head, "Never mind, are you ready to go?"

Jared chuckled and nodded at her dad and her mom, "We won't be out very late," he said and Christine literally dragged him out of the house.

"Are you okay?" he asked with a hint of humor in his voice.

"Do I look okay?" she chirped.

"You look fine to me."

Her internal thermometer was about to pop. The way he looked at her when he said she looked fine made her feel all warm and fuzzy inside. She reminded herself that she wasn't a teenager on a first date and forced to compose herself.

"I'm sorry, I just, I haven't been on a date in ages," she said as he opened the passenger door for her.

"Well that makes two of us, so trust me, there's no need to be nervous."

That was a relief she thought, but still, her heart kept thrumming against her chest.

Jarod had surprised her with a visit to a local musical arts theater, where they were hosting a fundraiser for a little girl who needed a skin graph after having sustained serious burns when she was caught in a burning car. Again, he had completely swept her feet out from under her, and she was in complete awe by how passionate he was.

"So do you always get involved in these fundraisers?" she asked curiously over dessert.

He chuckled and reached to wipe a smudge of cream from her chin, "Not always, it depends on the nature of the campaign. Sarah has a special place in my heart, she was only four when the car they were traveling in was involved in a head-on collision. Besides the fact that she was trapped in the burning car, she lost both her parents."

Christine swallowed at the lump in her throat, "That's terrible; I can't even begin to imagine how hard that must be for her."

This was exactly what she couldn't understand, why God would allow such a thing to happen, was just too cruel to comprehend.

"There's actually more to the story than most would believe," he said quietly, "You see, her parents were both alcoholics, and there were a few cases of child abuse against them, but the system failed her. But the funny thing is, after the accident, the driver of the other car, who survived, decided to adopt her and they are paying for all her medical bills."

Christine's jaw dropped and she blinked at the tears that threatened to spill.

"That's nothing short of a miracle," she said softly.

"You can say that again. It's true, God works in mysterious ways, and we don't always know the answers, but He does."

She was both shocked and thrilled by the news, and she couldn't help but cry. Jarod shifted his chair closer to hers and wrapped his arm around her shoulder.

"I didn't mean to make you cry, this is supposed to be the first date," he whispered.

"You didn't make me cry, it's just that," she sniffed against his shoulder, "all this time I figured God was merciless, never once did I consider a bigger picture."

"Shhh," Jarod comforted her and held her close, "It sometimes takes an extraordinary event to make us see things through His eyes, and all I know is that God never fails us, it's only our own expectations."

Chapter 6

Christine took a deep steadying breath as she stood at the end of the aisle, her dad by her side, and Jarod waiting in front, wearing his step out fireman's uniform with all his decorated medals. To the left were all his mates, and the entire squadron of firefighters some wearing their uniforms, other also wearing step outs, to the right was her family and some of her colleagues.

Her big day had arrived; she was finally going to promise herself to the one man she was willing to trust with her life. The wedding march started and she counted her steps in her mind, like a waltz down the aisle.

"I'm so proud to be your father," her dad whispered without moving his lips.

"Daddy you make me proud," she said, "thank you for introducing me to Jared."

Her insides were a kaleidoscope of butterflies and as her father handed her over to her future husband, she couldn't her fingers from trembling, but Jared took her hands in his and smiled at her. His eyes mirrored the same love she felt, and instantly he calmed her down.

It was a day to remember, Christine had not only promised herself to the love of her life, she also found God somewhere in the mix. Somewhere along the line, she realized that God never left; all she had to do was turn around and call on Him.

Christine and Jared lived happily ever after, doing what they both loved and in each other, they found the missing puzzle pieces that made them both complete.

"Are we going to go for green or yellow?" Christine asked holding up two cans of paint.

"Why not do both," Jared said as he worked at assembling the crib.

"Mmm, good point," she said and placed the two small tins on the coffee table, "how is the crib coming along?"

Jared stood up discarding the spanner and pulled his pregnant wife into his arms, "I think we just get our baby to share our bed for a while," he chuckled.

Christine laughed and wrapped her arms around her husband's neck, "I love you," she murmured against his lips.

"And I love you, Christine Marks," Jared said and kissed her.